TEVERTON HALL

By the same author

Ladysmead

TEVERTON HALL

JANE GILLESPIE

St. Martin's Press
New York

Library of Congress Cataloging in Publication Data

Gillespie, Jane, 1923-
  Teverton Hall.

  I. Title.
PR6057.I574T4   1984   823'.914   83-22929
ISBN 0-312-79371-5

First published in Great Britain in 1983 by Robert Hale Limited

First U.S. Edition

10 9 8 7 6 5 4 3 2 1

ONE

In the main street of Fraxted, a pleasant market town in Essex, stood a fine modern building beside whose entrance a well-polished brass plate held the legend: "Pavey and Son. Solicitors". The father of the present Mr Pavey had built the house and founded the firm. The law offices occupied the ground floor, and the upper floors provided commodious dwelling space for Mr Pavey's family, which was not large: he had one child only, a son named Robert.

Mr Pavey very much wished this son to enter the firm, and to sustain the accuracy of the brass plate's legend. He did not insist on this, since he did not want to force his son against his inclinations. Mr Pavey's own father had been of the despotic nature that considers no one else's inclinations, and there had been no question of Mr Pavey's being anything other than an appendage to the brass plate. Mr Pavey had found a solicitor's work pleasant enough – more especially since his father's decease – but, having suffered tyranny himself, was the more disposed to treat his own son with gentleness. Robert had been brought up by persuasion and example, rather than by constraint and punishment. Of the latter, there had been very little need. Robert Pavey was a docile and contented child and took it as assured that he would enter Pavey and Son as soon as he had completed his university studies. The only anxiety Mr Pavey might have entertained about his son was that Robert caused so little anxiety.

In temperament, Robert may have inherited from his mother a readiness to find life agreeable. Mrs Pavey, daughter of a local doctor, had been an unusually pretty girl, and yet without personal vanity, which combination of attributes made it seem to her that happiness bestowed itself upon her without any exertion on her part. It was through no deserving of her own, she felt, that she had been chosen by the highly eligible young Mr Pavey from among the belles of the neighbourhood; or that her domestic life was so tranquil, and Robert such a good boy, and everyone so kind to her. Untroubled even by excess of gratitude, she sat at her drawing-room window and watched the life of the town pass below her, with a mild untiring interest.

It was only when Robert returned home from Oxford that he was revealed to have offended: his debts followed him; he had exceeded his allowance. He was deeply apologetic and contrite. He would have been much surprised to know that this lapse gratified his father. Mr Pavey felt a sort of relief, that Robert should have put himself at fault, and was disposed to be lenient.

"I do not know how I came to spend so much," Robert protested. "I did try to keep my accounts, but, somehow, there seemed never to be enough time to reckon them up. The tailor's, I know now I was wrong about – It was just that all the other men were ordering new capes for the visit to Woodstock – You know how it is, sir – At least, I suppose you do not. At my age, you were steadier and more regardful of your parents –"

"Whatever my follies at your age, I have conveniently forgotten them," said Mr Pavey smiling. "And, Robert, your mother and I have never found you unregardful of us. I intended that you should enjoy your life at Oxford, and I am glad that you did."

"I did, sir, indeed. But I need not have been so extravagant –"

"Whatever your extravagances, they have led you into no vices. I am only afraid, Robert, that you are sometimes too easily led, in your friendliness and your enthusiasm. Sorry as you must be to part from your Oxford friends, you may be better away from their influence, and under the direction of your own judgement. Let us hope only that you will not find life at Fraxted too dull, after their society –"

"I am sure I shall not. I shall be glad to settle to work, sir."

Mr Pavey was pleased to hear this. When Robert added that he would save his money until he was able to pay all his debts, his father said:

"Come, let us hear no more about debts. Why have I myself saved some money, if not to rescue my only child from misfortunes? Your tailor and his like shall be paid off directly, and we shall say no more of it."

Robert's gratitude was sufficient to prepare his mind for the most diligent application to the affairs of Pavey and Son, as well as for the supposedly dull society of Fraxted. This was just as his father had intended. He was not sorry that Robert should begin his career at some slight sense of disadvantage, for which he fully intended his own kindness to compensate. The hint about Robert's being easily led, however, he had inserted into their conversation with the hope that it too would lodge in Robert's mind to some effect, though Mr Pavey preferred not to be too specific about it.

It happened that Robert had already some friends in the region of Fraxted who were all too likely to relieve its dullness, and Mr Pavey would have been glad if Robert, in his amendment of life, could let his intercourse with them dwindle. It was not in Mr Pavey's nature to dictate his son's choice of associates; and moreover, the family in question dealt with Pavey and Son in their legal affairs, which, as these were always in confusion, brought a great deal of business to the firm, besides making a rift between the families a potential embarrassment.

Not only the legal affairs of the Dallow family were in continual confusion. Their house, a large manor about a mile from the town, was all day in a bustle of someone looking for something or someone, of doors swinging open and voices raised. The countryside in all seasons was scattered with Dallow children on galloping ponies, the girls as vigorous and noisy as the boys. They were handsome and lively young people, but allowed to range free and unchecked. Their father was rarely at home, since his chief interest was the collection of antiquities, involving him in foreign travel for many months of each year. The eldest son, George Dallow, was by now grown old enough to take up the management of the estate that his father neglected; but for as far as Mr Pavey could see, George Dallow had no interest in anything beyond his own pleasure. Given horses and guns enough, he could amuse himself with no desire for responsibility. In his addiction to horse-racing he had acquired debts that made, besides inroads on the family finances, trifles of Robert Pavey's Oxford extravagances; which, naturally, Mr Pavey did not mention to his son.

George Dallow was about two years older than Robert and had from childhood been Robert's hero. Any mischief Robert had committed, he had been drawn into by George; anything Robert had wanted, from a fishing-rod to a faster pony, had been in order to be more like George. Robert had been accustomed to running in and out of the manor-house and adding to its commotion. In boyhood, this had been well enough; Mr Pavey had been pleased to have Robert spared some of the loneliness of an only child. But he foresaw that, as young men, Robert and George were too much dissimilar in station – and, he hoped, ultimately in tastes – to make a persisting friendship to Robert's advantage.

Robert's mother agreed with her husband over this, adding: "It would not be a good thing either, if Robert were to fall in love with one of those Dallow girls. I fancy they are all spoiled and giddy."

"Oh, come, my dear, let us not look as far ahead as that. He has shown no sign of affection for them. Indeed, do you remember that he pushed Miss Jane into the duckpond? And he told us that Miss Philippa has hair like an ill-tied cornsheaf."

Mrs Pavey gave her husband a wise and pitying glance. "Ah yes. But those were childish romps. Little girls, even hoydens like the Miss Dallows, become young women in time. Indeed, at the Assembly Room last week, at the concert, I thought Miss Dallow very pretty. While she was listening to the music, and forced to keep herself quiet and still, she was almost elegant. That blue gown suited her well. And you can be sure that, were Miss Philippa to have her hair nicely dressed, Robert would find its golden colour beautiful."

"I hope we need not fear that Robert will fall in love merely with beautiful golden hair," replied Mr Pavey, drawing upon himself another sagacious glance from his wife, whose own golden locks had so much attracted him twenty-five years ago. "Nor do I think we need concern ourselves immediately with his love life. His work comes first."

Robert himself intended that it should. He settled to his desk in the office with application and goodwill. It was perhaps unfortunate that the office's windows were situated as they were; the events of Fraxted displayed themselves outside, and no legal document could rival the departure of the London stage, or the spectacle of George Dallow clattering up the High Street in a brand new curricle. Mr Grimsby, the chief clerk, felt obliged to mention this when Mr Pavey made discreet inquiries after his son's progress.

Mr Pavey urged Mr Grimsby to make allowances, while not allowing himself any favouritism; he considered the question and reflected that Robert was, besides the son of the firm, the only member of it who was under the age of forty. The work Robert might sometimes find dull, but the company of such elderly colleagues might equally lack stimulus. Concern for Robert's welfare made Mr Pavey reconsider a request that he had lately received and had intended to reject: that he take an articled pupil into the firm.

The request had come from the clergyman of the Dallows' village, on behalf of his son. From the letter, it appeared that the clergyman could not afford a university education for the boy and was convinced that the legal profession would be most suitable to his own desires and his son's aptitudes. The letter was written in the most deferential language, declaring the writer to be fully aware of his own importunity in approaching Mr Pavey, his only excuse being that he had heard Mr Pavey everywhere praised as a model of generosity and legal pre-eminence. It described the writer's son as outstandingly diligent, sober and anxious in every way to please; Mr Pavey would never regret his condescension in accepting him as a pupil.

Condescension or no, Mr Pavey now decided that life might be more pleasant for Robert with a younger face about the office; nor was he above imagining that, were this young man as diligent as his father said, he might set Robert an example. So Mr Pavey wrote in his own hand to the Rector of Teverton, suggesting that his son be sent for an interview.

TWO

The Rectory at Teverton stood at some distance from the manor-house, closer to the small village with its duckpond in which Robert Pavey had once immersed one of the manor's daughters. At the Rectory, all was tidiness and decorum. The Rector himself worked in the garden to produce fruit and vegetables, useful to the domestic budget and gratifying to the prospect from his book-room window.

Into this room he summoned his son William, as soon as Mr Pavey's letter had been received. "I am overjoyed," he said when he had read the letter aloud, "that my application has, after only a few weeks, met with such a gracious acknowledgement. I know that you too, William, must be delighted by the affability with which Mr Pavey expresses himself."

"Yes, sir," William said.

" 'Yes, sir'? Is that all you can find to say, when a man of Mr Pavey's position makes the time among all his onerous duties to offer you an interview? Let me remind you, William, that much may depend on this interview and the manner in which you conduct yourself. Let me remind you again, as so often I must, I am afraid, of the importance of ready and obliging speech in all relationships, and especially in those in which one occupies the subordinate position. Nothing so well recommends a man to those who are able to bestow favours upon him, as a well-turned compliment or phrase of respectful admiration. Gratitude can not be expressed too frequently, nor praise of a benefactor's kindness too fully; provided that this is done with due deference and humility.''

Mr Collins, the Rector, had a high opinion of his own humility. He paused to regard William who, about to say 'Yes, sir' again, remembered its inadequacy, so, in default of anything else, remained silent.

"You, William" remarked his father in reproach, "are tongue-tied.''

"Yes, sir," admitted William. Then he bit his lip, blushing, and gazed out of the window at the scarlet blossoms of the runner beans.

"It disappoints me," Mr Collins continued, "to note you still so lacking in the normal social graces, when I have been to such expense to give you the best I can in the way of an education. A school like yours, you must understand, made great demands on my purse." He paused, then went on: "No, I do not expect gratitude. I must reconcile myself, I see, to doing my duty as a father and a Christian and receiving no thanks for it. I stand self-rebuked for expecting thanks. Be that as it may, I regret that I am not in a position to extend your education further. Nothing would have pleased me more than to see you receive ordination like myself. It is a calling of the highest respectability. You are my only son, and I owe it to myself to do all in my power to further and assist you. I shall myself write a letter for you to copy out, neatly, in reply to this of Mr Pavey's. I shall suggest that I accompany you to the interview. Were you to suffer one of your tongue-tied fits upon that occasion, it would ruin my hopes of launching you upon a valuable and lucrative, and not unworthy, profession. Opportunities such as this, William, are not to be missed on account of your awkwardness and unreadiness. I can face no more disappointments. My life, as you know, suffers already under such severe and constant disappointments, that to have my son added to them would be more than fortitude could be expected to survive."

William, whose face was now equal in scarlet to the bean blossoms, did indeed know of the disappointments in his father's life, but he was not equal to commiseration; he remained tongue-tied.

There had been two major misfortunes affecting Mr Collins, not the less because he was innocent of their occurrence. The first of these concerned the patroness of his first living, from whom he had received every mark of favour, and to whom he had extended every mark of gratitude, until the aristocratic patroness's nephew married a connection of Mr Collins's. For this Mr Collins was in no way responsible; he had indeed advised against the match, knowing that his patroness would be incensed by this degradation of her nephew; he was dismayed when her anger was directed too against himself, and when she made this so evident that his parishioners scarcely dared attend his church.

In this plight, Mr Collins appealed even to the disgraced nephew for help; and he, rather than attempt mediation with his aunt, sought about for a living, having none then at his own disposal; and through a friend, was able to offer Teverton, in Mr Dallow's gift. At that time, William's birth was expected and the infant's welfare was first in nearly all hearts. When the child was born he was christened Fitzwilliam in honour of the mismatched nephew, and Mr Collins addressed himself to his new patron with effusions of humble gratitude. But as time passed, and no further gestures were received from the nephew, and the Rectory and garden were found to be smaller and less convenient than those in Kent, and Mr Dallow found to be less susceptible to respectful adulation than his precursor (being in any case for most of the year in Asia) and it was understood that the nephew and aunt were again on fair terms, the boy's name was for convenience shortened to William, which was also his father's name; and Mr Collins recognised disappointment.

The second misfortune was equally unmerited. A distant cousin of Mr Collins possessed an estate in Hertfordshire which was entailed upon the male line of the family. This cousin had no sons, so the estate would devolve upon Mr Collins. Mr Collins did not form any immediate expectation of this, although his cousin was many years older than he. But again, as time passed, the suspense became harder to bear. His cousin's daughters were all married and dispersed and, since his wife's death, he seemed to spend all his time visiting in Derbyshire or London. "And there," Mr Collins complained to his family, "the house stands unoccupied while I have to cram myself into this inconsiderable little Rectory. And who is maintaining the estate? It will be worth nothing when I inherit it. And my cousin appears to be in excellent health and will probably remain so – Not, naturally, that I would wish otherwise –"

"Naturally not, my love," Mrs Collins reassured him.

"– And I and my family remain deprived of what in justice I could call our rightful property, neglected by all the members of *that* family, wealthy as they are, and cordial as has been my attitude to them. It was I who first extended the olive branch, and sought to heal the breach caused by the wretched business of the entail."

He had sought to do so, in that instance, by marrying one of his cousin's daughters, but of this he did not often remind Mrs Collins, and if he did, she overlooked his lapse of tact. The chosen young cousin had rejected him, which had been to the advantage of Mrs Collins, a neighbour and close friend; she had been available to sympathise, and to soothe his just resentment against his cousin's family, until he observed that she would make an excellent wife; and since his patroness had commanded him to marry, and he did not wish to return unaffianced to Kent, he had swiftly redirected his affections; nor were they of such quality that he had since regretted it. Mrs Collins's widowed mother and two married sisters still lived in the same part of Hertfordshire, and she was able to give him their news of the estate and to report that it was not neglected; which tidings Mr Collins did not always find acceptable.

"Maria writes that they have built a new barn behind the farm —"

"I wonder if it was necessary. All such expenses must be a drain on the resources. It sounds to me like a reckless outlay —"

"And they have felled the big elms on the west side of the drive."

"No doubt selling the timber at a great price, which my cousin will pocket —"

"Maria says they were in a dangerous condition, and that is why —"

"As I thought. The place is being allowed to deteriorate. It makes great demands on my fortitude, to stand by and allow others to do as they please with the property. And what of William? All the tender feelings of a father are provoked, when I have to deny him the opportunities he needs at his stage of life. And what of Marcia? She will soon be of an age to marry. What provision can we make for her, in all this uncertainty? The worry of it sometimes threatens to overcome me."

Mrs Collins entered into no argument of the matter, but saw to it, with domestic comforts and encouragement in his gardening, that her husband was never entirely overcome. The disappointments did not weigh upon her except as they affected her husband. She had at no time formed high expectations of life and was happy in the daily governance of her household and in the company of her children. It was of such matters that she wrote to her husband's married cousins, with whom she had remained friendly. Mr Collins did not view this correspondence with favour, and would have done so with less, had he known that Mrs Collins did not include in it the plaints and compliments that he required her to; these, with her own fortitude, she kept to herself.

THREE

William Collins hated his own stupidity, especially when he was in the company of his father. He did not understand how it was that he could not find a word to say for himself, when he had the example of his father's impressive command of phrase. Nor could he understand how it was that he could not imitate his father's dignified command of a social encounter. As a small boy he had revered his father during the church services, fearing that he himself would never be worthy of the clerical profession. Even so, he was now eighteen years old and should not have been frightened half out of his wits by the prospect of an interview with Mr Pavey. He was grateful that his father accompanied him to the interview, during which William was as tongue-tied as they both had feared, and he was certain that, had his father not been present, Mr Pavey would not have been persuaded to take William as a pupil.

This was probably so, but not for the reasons William suspected. Mr Pavey said later: "He appears a pleasant enough boy, although I had no chance of estimating his ability. With such a father, I wonder if he has had any such chance himself. If he does not prove apt, I shall of course not sign the articles; but for the present we shall take him on, if only to deliver him from the reverend gentleman's paternal solicitude. Robert, you must look after young

Collins in the office, and not let Grimsby frighten him."

"But Grimsby frightens me, Father."

"It might be as well if occasionally he did. It is strange," continued Mr Pavey, "that, living as close as Teverton, Mr Collins has not crossed my path hitherto."

"I expect you have seen him in the town, but had no reason to notice him. The Dallows know him, of course," Robert added. "They attend his church. George says he is a prosy old nuisance, always trying to call upon them at the Hall."

"I am obliged to you for Mr George Dallow's opinion."

"Having met Mr Collins yourself, Father, you may sympathise with it."

"Yes, yes. I do not imply that Mr George Dallow is the poorer judge of clergymen for his being an excellent judge of horses."

Mrs Pavey, who had as usual observed all comings and goings from her drawing-room window, now offered: "I have seen Mr Collins and his family many times, though we have not been introduced, I think. Mrs Collins brought her daughter to the last ball of the spring, in the Assembly Room. She is a sensible-looking woman, but neither of them was so well dressed that one would have stared. The girl – I do not remember her name – resembled her brother a little, in features."

"Poor girl," was Robert's comment.

Robert had not been present at William's interview, but had had a glimpse in the lobby of a solidly built and heavy-faced young man with fair hair. When he encountered the new pupil in their office a few days later, his impression of solemnity and slowness was confirmed. Robert could not seriously suppose that anyone could be frightened by Mr Grimsby, much less by himself. He could not suspect that his own cheerful conversation rendered William as tongue-tied as Mr Grimsby's stern silence rendered him apprehensive William was in a rigor of fear for most of his first weeks with Pavey and Son. His tied tongue protruded from his mouth in his anxiety to make no mistake in the conveyance deed he had been set to copy, and when Robert from his own desk sang out: "Look – Here comes old Miss Parkinson in a freak of a new bonnet!" William's dilemma, between offending Mr Grimsby by looking out of the window or offending Mr Robert by not looking out of the window, was painful.

After a little time, a tacit alliance developed between these two young members of the staff. William marvelled at Robert's audacity, even in the son of the firm; and Robert marvelled at William's diligence, even in a probationary pupil. Robert found that William could be depended upon to help him out if he fell behind with his work, and William found that Robert could be depended upon to laugh off any error William might make, deflecting the reproof of Mr Grimsby. To make William laugh was beyond Robert's power, but William listened with serious attention to tales of the gay life of Oxford, which Robert found not unflattering. And William, in private, found it not unflattering that he was given a nickname by Mr Robert.

This came about when the articles were to be signed, and William's full name thereby revealed. "Fitzwilliam, I declare! Why have you kept such a distinction from us?" cried Robert in amusement. "I shall address you as Fitz in future. Shall you not like that?

"You must call me by any name you wish, Mr Robert," said William. He saw nothing amusing in his name, but understood that Mr Robert was not intending to mock him.

"Then, if you are to address me as *I* wish, please let us have no more of 'Mr' Robert. I am not yet ready to be considered as venerable as Mr Grimface in your eyes."

"I think you mean Mr Grims*by*, Mr Robert," William reminded him.

"To be sure I do, Mr Fitz. What a careless slip of the tongue. How good of you to point it out to me."

In this tone, even William divined mockery, and blushed, confused. Robert clapped him on the shoulder exclaiming: "Pay no attention to my nonsense, Fitz. Do you not, though, find this office often dull?"

"Indeed I do not, Mr – Robert," William assured him.

"Well, you are a good fellow, and if I could once prevail upon you to laugh at Mr Grimface, I beg his pardon, Mr Grimchin, you and I would fast become friends."

As it was, the work of the firm was proceeding well with the inclusion of its two junior members and Mr Pavey was able to congratulate himself on the ease of Robert's absorption into it. By and by he had no hesitation in allowing Robert days of freedom in which to go shooting or hunting with George Dallow; Robert promised his father: "My work will not suffer for it, sir," adding to himself: Fitz will see to it that it does not. Apart from these diversions, life passed without incident for about two years and everyone seemed content.

Everyone, that is, excepting Mr Collins. The pasage of time brought him only prolonged disappointment and rendered him increasingly querulous. He heard no news of failing health in his elderly cousin and himself failed to recommend himself to his patron during Mr Dallow's infrequent periods of residence at Teverton. Nor did his son give him any assistance by advancing in acquaintance with the family of his employer, much less with the family at Teverton Hall.

"You owe it to yourself, William" Mr Collins complained, "even be you not aware of owing it to me, to make all approaches possible to those who may further your interests. There are innumerable little ways in which pleasing and acceptable attentions can be offered, and I have suggested many to you, but you are apparently unwilling – I dare not say unable – to undertake such missions. I have done what I can, in repeatedly expressing to Mr Pavey, when I chance to meet him in the town, my gratitude on your behalf, together with compliments to his wife, and all due awareness of obligation, which could more properly come from you. In view of the dignity of my cloth alone, it would not be too much to expect the Paveys at least to invite us to drink tea. Mr Robert Pavey is not, by virtue of his father's standing, so far above you by virtue of your own father's calling, that the two of you should not associate on terms of friendship. And you tell me he is much at Teverton Hall. I shall not cease to be assiduous in my own courtesies in that direction, but were you to exert a more ready spirit, it should not be impossible for you to secure an invitation there through Mr Robert. I look to you to achieve this."

"Yes, sir," answered William, wholly daunted by such a notion.

It did now and then happen that Robert Pavey set out to visit his friends at Teverton when his day's work was ended, and, were the weather bad and he driving instead of riding, he would offer a seat to Fitz, to save him from the wet mile between Fraxted and the Rectory. Then they spoke of the Dallows, about whom William felt some curiosity.

"Miss Philippa is the youngest, is she not?"

"No; I believe Walter is twelve months younger than she," Robert replied. "Corinna is the eldest of the girls, and I know she is the same age as myself. They are delightful people, all of them, and have more life about them than anyone else in this neighbourhood. And they are all clever. There is nothing George could not do, if he set his mind to it.

The girls are grown very handsome, do you not think?"

"I am sure they are, though I see them only from a distance, or in church. They seem to me to resemble each other closely. My father," added William, innocently, "wishes me to become acquainted with them, I know."

"Well, and so you will, I dare say, since they live so close to you," said Robert, reining in his horse to let William alight at the Rectory gate. "Good-night, Fitz; I shall see you tomorrow," he called, driving on before William could summon any pleasing or acceptable expressions of gratitude for his ride.

FOUR

It was at about this time that someone else began, like Mr Collins, to find the passage of time unprofitable. Corinna Dallow, eldest daughter of the manor, wondered at last whether her whole life might not soon waste itself away in rustic pleasures; something — she knew not quite what — was missing, and at this rate might miss her altogether.

In her heart, she knew well enough what any handsome and lively young woman of almost three and twenty desires. She knew that she ought to go more into society and seek a position in the wider world suitable to her birth and gifts; but there was little to attract her in Fraxted; the concerts and balls of the Assembly Room set a constraint upon her natural energy. She loved music and dancing, but hated to sit still or to be stiffly polite.

Constraint of any kind was repugnant to all the Miss Dallows. There had been no lack of propriety in their upbringing, but only an unusual amount of freedom. Mrs Pavey was not exact in calling them 'spoiled'; a fitter word might have been 'untamed'. They were all three vivacious, affectionate, pretty girls and easily mastered such accomplishments as appealed to them. They were alike in tastes, as in appearance; any distant observer such as William Collins could have been excused for failing to tell them apart. They, and their two brothers, had all the dark golden hair that Robert Pavey likened to corn, brilliant hazel eyes and glowing complexions. They looked, and were, eminently healthy; and this their mother viewed with tentative satisfaction, for the health of her children was the principal concern of her life.

Mrs Dallow had been the daughter of a diplomat and spent most of her youth in foreign countries, so that she saw nothing unusual in her husband's habit of travelling abroad. When they married, and Mr Dallow inherited Teverton Hall, their first two children died in infancy. This caused Mrs Dallow such distress that she could reckon nothing in the world as important as the survival of their successors. As long as her five remaining children were well, she asked nothing more for herself or for them. The constitutions of these children were naturally robust; indeed they had need to be, for, far from cosseting them, their anxious mother submitted them to one severe regimen after another, according as she discovered new medical books or heard of additional diseases and their remedies. She had faith in any specific, provided it was new to her, and when she heard of any new illness, could not rest until she had applied every means of averting it. Fortunately, she had retained her faith in the London doctor who, soon after the birth of George, had advised a strong diet and outdoor exercise as the basis of well-being. All the Dallow children liked nothing better than exerting themselves out of doors, and all ate heartily, which may have fortified them against the herbal infusions, embrocations, hot and cold spongings and other measures they were submitted to. The normal childhood ailments affected them lightly; they had to fall out of high trees or off galloping ponies before they were laid low; but even broken bones knit quickly in these splendidly fit young creatures.

Even at this date, Mrs Dallow found fresh sources of

alarm. She had read in a manual that flecks of white beneath the fingernails could be an indication of deficiency in the marrow of the bones, and all her family had to attend twice daily for her inspection of their fingernails. This they did with good humour, for they indulged their mother in her whims as she indulged them in their exploits. Mrs Dallow had always been used to suppose that, were there noise enough about the house, her family must be in proportion alive. It may not be surprising that on account of this maternal surveillance mixed with liberty, and on account of the prolonged absences of their father, and their own happiness in each other's company, the young Dallows had formed a self-sufficient group, and if they suffered from any potential threat, it was that of an unduly prolonged childhood.

Corinna was becoming aware of this. She was still happy in the pursuits that she and her sisters enjoyed: they rode, walked, gathered berries and experimented in the making of preserves, vied with each other in drawing crayon portraits of their dogs and, in the evenings at the hearth, put out the candles and told each other ghost stories. They did read books, but their restless energies must seize upon the tales to be acted out; dressing up, they performed the most horrifying scenes (usually taking place in a haunted abbey) with dramatic screamings and faintings in the halls and stairways of the manor.

Caring nothing for what the world thought, Corinna did not wonder whether the world might find her style of life unbefitting the dignity of Miss Dallow of Teverton Hall. A certain dignity in herself she felt to be wanting. She carried her complaints to her brother George.

"We are too much isolated here. We are not invited anywhere, and I imagine it is because we do not invite anyone. Why do we not entertain company? If my father were at home, he would arrange –"

"Yes, exactly so," George interrupted her, with a speed that showed a conscience already stirred. "In the absence of my father I dare not take it upon me to use his house for hospitality."

"I am sure he expects you to stand in his place, in regard to your sisters. You should feel responsible –"

"My dear sister, I have worries and responsibilities enough of my own. In any case, my father will soon be home again, and then he will invite Dr Ingle and his garrulous wife to dinner, for your benefit –"

"My father will not be at home until after the summer," protested Corinna, but, knowing that further protest to George would be ineffective, she desisted, hoping only that her father might remain with them for some months and render this next winter more eventful than the last. Mr Dallow was as energetic as his children and as swift to action as he was to decision. As soon as the family met at dinner, on the day of his return from Constantinople, he was ready to listen to Corinna's plea, and solicitous to answer:

"Yes, my dear, I can well believe that not much entertainment has been had here in my absence. But, George, what have you been about? While I am from home, you are the head of the family, and must look out for your mother and sisters. I have troubles enough in my own work, and cannot govern from a distance the affairs of Teverton."

"I did not want to make free with your house, sir –"

"Nonsense," returned Mr Dallow in his brisk tone. "You are as free as you wish to be, and you know it. You have never hesitated to make free with my stables or coverts."

George was a little abashed at this, but Mrs Dallow was calling:

"My love, you have been two hours now in the house,

and not yet asked after the health of the children."

"I see little need of that," said Mr Dallow, glancing round the table at the radiant faces of his family. To please Mrs Dallow he added: "They are all well, I trust?"

"Pretty well, though Philippa lost two pounds in weight during June, and Walter started with a cough, which he pretended was only from the dust of the threshing-floor."

"Well, and so I expect it was," said Mr Dallow, resuming without ceremony his own train of thought. "So Corinna wishes to receive company? I have no objection. There are many neighbours whom I ought to meet while I am at home. I grow out of touch. Is Sir Edgar Bewley still in London? We should invite him and his daughters. They will like to dance, I suppose? Let us give a ball. A modest affair, of course, but we must do it soon. I have to go to Paris next month and thence to Rome, and may not be back before Christmas."

The Bewleys, it was heard, were not yet come down into the country, nor had the season of balls yet arrived, but an informal dance was planned at Teverton at short notice. On a warm afternoon of early autumn, George Dallow made this announcement to Robert Pavey, by the informal means of tapping at the window of Pavey and Son with his riding-cane. Robert leapt from his desk and threw up the sash.

"It is to be nothing grand," George explained. "Twelve or sixteen couples only. You must come; and I am supposed to think of others. I cannot. The Websters – our cousins from Bath, you know – are asked to visit for the occasion, but that will make only nine couples. Must we have Bernard Phillips? Now think, Robert, of others?"

On a generous impulse Robert said: "Why do you not invite Fitz and his sister?"

"Who in the world are they?"

"Oh, you know, the Collinses, son and daughter of your

Rector."

"Oh, those. Do you imagine they can dance?"

Robert tried to make it clear, by a rolling of his eyes and backward jerk of his head, that George's voice must be audible within the office.

"What is the matter?" inquired George amazed.

"You remember that Fitz – that is, William Collins – is here in the firm now, so that I can give him your invitation," said Robert, loudly.

"Well, no, I did not. I thought you had the toothache. Yes," added George recollecting himself, "we should be happy to see Mr and Miss Collins at our dance. But," he could not resist adding again as he turned away, "no parents, please, on that evening."

Robert closing the window observed that William's face, bent as usual over his work, was scarlet. Robert could find no apology to make for George, nor did he understand that William was discomfited only by having heard himself mentioned by Mr George Dallow, and by the prospect of an invitation to Teverton Hall. That Mr George Dallow should not imagine him or Marcia capable of dancing did not at all surprise him. The final instruction that there were to be 'no parents' at the dance only increased his alarm. He walked home in trepidation and stood at the window of his mother's drawing-room summoning courage to mention the invitation. His father was outside, gathering windfall apples into a basket. William, as twilight too gathered, was still watching, when there was a sound of hooves in the lane. Mr Collins set down his basket and went to the gate, to meet a servant from the manor who handed him a letter. George Dallow, repentant of his gracelessness, had gone home to urge his mother to write the invitation that Mr Collins, narrowing his eyes in the fading light, read carefully, before retrieving his basket and coming indoors.

"This," he announced, entering the drawing-room, "is addressed, to my surprise, to you and Marcia, William. Observing that it came from the Hall, I assumed it to be for myself. Indeed I cannot believe that it is not. I cannot conceive that, while Mr Dallow himself is in residence, any invitation from that quarter should not be extended to me. I must call upon all my reserves of charity, not to allow myself to suspect a slight."

"What invitation are you speaking of?" asked Mrs Collins.

"This is an invitation to an informal ball, to take place on Friday week. It is written by Mrs Dallow. – Depend upon it, however, this is a mere oversight on her part. She has omitted to prefix my name with its due title. In her haste, she forgot to write *The Reverend* William Collins. I can forgive her that small carelessness. I appreciate the gesture of the invitation, long overdue though I must admit it to be, and shall reply at once, in terms that indicate nothing but that appreciation."

Here William was compelled to explain, in a mumble, that he had known of the invitation, and that it was extended only to Marcia and himself. His father was still incredulous.

"You have misunderstood what Mr George and Mr Robert have told you, in your stupid fashion, William. Can it be possible, my love," he appealed to Mrs Collins, "that the Dallows should deliberately overlook me – and you – after all the courtesies I have been at pains to show them?"

"It is perfectly possible," replied Mrs Collins, in the equable tone with which she was used to soothe her husband, "that the Dallows should give a small party for the young people only. I expect we shall hear that other parents – Mr and Mrs Pavey, for example – are not invited." Her attention was already turned, according to her nature, upon practical matters. There had been some muslin with lilac sprigs in Thompson's in Fraxted which would make a very pretty gown for Marcia, had the shop a sufficient length of it. "Friday week, I think you said?"

"Yes; I suppose that could be so. Is it so, William? Is the ball for a few children of the neighbourhood only? You must discover that from Mr Robert as soon as you may. Meanwhile, you must write a suitably grateful reply to Mrs Dallow. I shall dictate it to you."

"I am not sure that I want to go to the ball, Father."

"What you want, or do not want, is nothing to do with the matter. Your duty is plain. You will be standing in my place, and owe it to me to make a pleasing impression upon the Dallows. An informal dance is no great affair. It should not be beyond your powers to conduct yourself as befits my standing. I am not to be disappointed in you, William."

William was much afraid that he was, and his face hardened between terror and obstinacy. Mrs Collins said to him in a gentle tone:

"I dare say, William, that Marcia will be glad to go."

At this, William, who was fond of his sister and willing to give her pleasure, recognised a more welcome duty. "Very well then, I shall go," he agreed. "Even though I shall hate every minute."

"Your language is disrespectful, sir," his father reproved him, "and your manner ungracious. I am ashamed of you. Do not let me hear you speak so again, of those who show you condescension and favour. Go and bring your writing-paper at once."

Without any joy of anticipation, William penned his father's phrases describing his joyful anticipation of the ball. Nor was he greatly cheered, when he and Marcia were alone later, to hear that she did not look forward to the evening more than he.

"I am frightened by the idea of going among so many strangers, without even my mother."

"But I shall be with you, Marcia."

"You are a little frightened yourself, William, were you to admit it."

He could not deny it, but he tried to comfort her: "They will not all be strangers. And you know that you enjoy dancing."

"So I do. But no one will ask to dance with me, you know."

Marcia Collins had just passed her eighteenth birthday and had for two winters attended some of the public balls in Fraxted, where she had attracted small attention, nor expected any. As a little girl she had been heavy and plain, but had not been encouraged to dwell upon her appearance. Mr Collins deplored all vanities in young girls, and Mrs Collins had had no pretensions to beauty herself, so felt other values to be more worth the cultivation. At eighteen, Marcia's figure had grown more slender, and her features, though still strongly formed, were regular, and her complexion fine. She was now a pleasant-looking girl and had inherited much of her mother's good sense and intelligence. She had been constantly in her mother's company and shared Mrs Collins's interest in good books and music, as well as in the efficient running of a household. Possibly Mrs Collins had erred in keeping her daughter, in her own isolation, so much by her, because although Marcia's mind was well developed, she was still timid in society. She held her father in as high a reverence as did William and was neither surprised nor disappointed when he pronounced that a new gown for the Dallows' ball was beyond his means. But when Mrs Collins, after appearing to ponder the question, suggested that for Marcia to be freshly dressed might be interpreted as a mark of respect for the Dallows, Mr Collins at once agreed, urging Marcia to make herself as fine as possible.

Of this, Marcia had no high hope, but the lilac sprigged muslin was bought and as she stitched at its seams she tried to bear in mind her father's comment that an informal dance was no great affair. She did not suppose that it was; only, some intuition warned her that there was a hidden significance about this one. The young Dallows, whom she knew well by sight, having all her life seen them flying by on their ponies or fidgeting in church, she might now be about to meet on a new footing. She could console herself only with the hope that William would not enjoy the dance any more than she and might be prepared to bring her home early.

FIVE

On the evening of Friday week, Robert Pavey called for the young Collinses in his father's carriage, since he was already conveying to the Dallows' ball two sisters from Fraxted. Robert perceived that Fitz and his sister were stiff and grave, unlike guests setting out for an enjoyable occasion; but they were alone in this; everyone else at Teverton was in the gayest of spirits. The large drawing-room had been cleared to permit space for the dancing of the twelve, sixteen or eighteen couples expected; no one was sure of the number, since the normal Dallow confusion had obtained in the arrangement of the party. All the normal Dallow enthusiasm, however, had, after days of uproar, rendered the rooms magnificent and the Dallow spendthriftiness had provided an abundant supper, a group of musicians from London, and banks of flowers in every corner. The Dallows themselves provided as admirable a display, the girls in elegant gowns, and the cousin from Bath, Henry Webster, resplendent in the dress uniform of a captain in the Third–Shires. He was to open the ball with Corinna and the set was already forming when Robert ushered his own company into the room. He looked about for Jane, whom he had engaged for the first dance, and for George, who was not to be seen. In so doing, he caught sight of a figure among the gathering dancers, to whom his eyes returned, his attention arrested. It was of a young girl in white, standing opposite Walter Dallow. She was delicately formed, with a sweet serenity of countenance as striking to Robert as the beauty of her features.

"Come, Robert," cried Jane Dallow tapping his head with her fan, "you are late. Hurry, let us take our place. I do not want to be lower in the set than Philippa and Bernard." She drew him across the room, barely ahead of her sister, as the music started. He was unable then to ask her the name of the young lady in white, or to give further thought to Fitz and his sister.

William, too slow to find a place for Marcia and himself in the set, was left beside her at the foot of the room. They alone were not dancing and, as dancing was the sole activity of the occasion, there were no gossips sitting along the walls, or strolling card-players, to conceal their isolation. "We shall join in, as soon as we can," William assured his sister, without confidence. The room was amazingly full, and no one offered to admit them to the set, though it seemed to them both that stray glances of indifferent curiosity were thrown towards them. Marcia murmured: "It does not matter, William. I am happy to watch," without daring to lift her eyes to do so.

It was at this juncture that George Dallow entered the room. He had for his own reasons allowed himself to be unavoidably detained in the stables, and this late appearance he had half intended to be a non-appearance; but, when he recollected that his parents had gone to such trouble to provide the entertainment, and that his sisters had so much looked forward to it, he repented of his churlishness and effected a rapid change of clothes and heart, preparing himself to make the best of the evening and perhaps contribute to its success.

Now the sound of the music, and the faces of the happy

dancers, roused all his natural amiability. Passing the pair of non-dancers by the door he promptly stopped, bowed and asked to have the honour of being presented to the lady and of asking her to dance. He gained admission to the set by thumping his brother upon the shoulder and crying: "Let us in, Walter, my boy!" as he pushed his way across, leading Marcia to her place.

So it came about, to Marcia's astonishment, that she found herself dancing with Mr George Dallow himself. The appraising stares she received as this was observed caused her some confusion; but her neighbour in the set, a very pretty girl in white, smiled at her in a welcoming manner, and George Dallow could not have been more easy and kind.

"Miss Collins?" he verified. "May I ask where you live?" And when she told him that she lived in Teverton's own Rectory, he exclaimed: "Do you indeed?" as if that interested him – nay, surprised him.

In truth George was surprised, that the daughter of the tedious Rector should be such a modest quiet girl and should dance so well. He had by now forgotten his unfortunate speech at Robert's office window, but felt that young Collins should still be in some way on his conscience; he was glad to have chanced upon this means of making reparation, by paying attention to the sister. Nor was it a hardship to George. Marcia, in the faint blush of shyness and in her crisp new muslin, was looking well; and as he began to explain to her what had delayed him – his mare had given birth to a sickly foal – she listened attentively, even raising her eyes to his in her concern for the little creature's struggle for life. It had been George's experience that ladies with whom one danced expected foolish compliments on their gowns and smirking small-talk. It was refreshing to be able to speak of horses and to have such a willing listener. William, watching them from the half-shelter of a bank of flowers, admired his sister's composure as well as her luck.

Before the dance ended Robert contrived to ask Jane: "Who is the lady dancing with Walter? I do not know her."

Jane laughed. "Oh, yes, you do. Is your heavy study of the law affecting your memory? You have seen her before, many times." As Robert remained perplexed, she conceded: "It is our cousin, Henry's little sister: Silvia Webster. Now do you remember?"

"I hardly do –"

"Well, please do not stand gaping like that. We shall hold up the dance."

"Forgive me. It was just that I was trying to recognise her –"

"And do you?"

Again Robert replied: "I hardly do. She is grown very – much."

"Yes, she is very ladylike now," agreed Jane as if catching at his meaning. "I suppose that is from the influence of the school in Bath, or of Mrs I-forget-her-name who has been her guardian."

"Is she to stay with you for any while?"

"It is still being talked of. Henry must rejoin his regiment in two days' time, but I see no excuse for Silvia to hurry away. As you may now recall, she was always anxious to do that."

Robert recalled quite well the circumstances of Silvia Webster, for he had handled some of the relevant documents in his father's office. There they had been, however, mere documents, and had not warned him of what Silvia Webster had become since he had last seen her in person, which must have been, he now reckoned, about five years ago. By now, she must be seventeen years old.

Henry and Silvia Webster were the children of a cousin of Mr Dallow's. They had been left orphans when Henry was thirteen years old and Silvia five. As they had no nearer relations, Mr Dallow had assumed their legal guardianship, which process had added to the work of Pavey and Son. It had at first been intended that the two children should live at Teverton; but Henry had been closely attached to a school friend whose parents wanted to have him during the school holidays; while Silvia, very small and miserable at the loss of her mother, had been overwhelmed by the boisterousness of her Dallow cousins and, in spite of their willingness to accept her, remained so withdrawn and fearful that even Mrs Dallow's ministrations could not reach her. She was sent to an elderly great-aunt in Bath, where she settled and improved, coming to Teverton only on visits which, as Jane remembered, she did not seem to enjoy. The great-aunt died when Silvia was fourteen, but still she remained in Bath, now in the care of a Mrs Forbes (whose name Jane had forgotten), a lady who had acted as companion to the great-aunt and had necessarily had much to do with Silvia's upbringing. The arrangements over the wills of the Webster parents and of the great-aunt, and over the allowance made to Mrs Forbes for Silvia's care and education, and over similar concerns for Henry, all formed part of that confusion that Mr Pavey could never keep Mr Dallow in England for long enough to resolve. "I leave it all in your capable hands, Pavey," he would say as his trunks were strapped, "and I shall sign whatever you want me to, as soon as I come back."

From the years preceding his own study of the Dallows' legal affairs, Robert remembered Silvia Webster as a pale nervous little girl, often a hindrance on the excursions he made with the young Dallows, lagging behind or becoming lost and frightened. "Where is Silvia? We must find her before we go home," had been the constant cry. A little later, he remembered Corinna's telling him: "Silvia is probably not coming back, and we are glad; but Mama is sorry, because she says Silvia needs the country air for her health." It did not now appear that Silvia's health had suffered in Bath. She was slight, but not thin; her fair skin held a tint of colour, and throughout the evening she danced as tirelessly as her cousins. She did not lack partners. Robert, growing inattentive to his own, at last followed George across the room to ask:

"Will you not introduce me to Miss Webster? I do not think she can remember me."

"Very well, if you wish it," said George with an unexpected lack of enthusiasm. Preceding Robert, and interrupting Miss Webster's talk with Bernard Phillips, he said: "Silvia, Robert Pavey does not think you remember him. You must excuse me – I would ask you to dance, but I have a sick horse I must visit. Perhaps Robert will dance with you in my place." With which, he departed.

Face to face with Miss Webster, Robert was overtaken with a strange awkwardness. When he repeated George's request for the dance, his voice stuttered. A dance had never seemed to him so brief. The touch of her light hand rendered him speechless, but towards the end of the set he forced himself to say:

"Will you be staying here for long?"

"I should like to stay for a while. The countryside is so beautiful at this time of year."

"It may be," went on Robert presently, "that you will appreciate it more than you used to, on your earlier visits?"

"I have always been fond of the country," said Miss Webster. "But if," with a slight smile, "you are suggesting that I shall be happier at Teverton than I used to be, then I think you are right."

"Were you not happy here?"

"You must remember what a stupid, over-cautious child I was."

"Indeed, I remember nothing of the kind."

"My cousins were very kind to me, but I did not respond. Now, I hope, I have grown braver."

Robert was endeavouring to frame a compliment, in contradiction of her self-deprecation, but the dance had ended. Another partner awaited her; as she turned away from Robert, he felt a keen disappointment, and a dissatisfaction with himself that was as strange as his awkwardness. He had not enjoyed this ball in the least; yet he wished it to go on for ever.

George Dallow had returned, and sought Marcia, to give her the good news that the little foal was gaining strength. "Will you dance?" he added, supposing that they might as well do so, while he described to her the animal's progress. So, again, Marcia was seen to be chosen by the son of the manor; and in the interim she had not been without partners. As a result of George's choosing her for the first dance, several young men of her passing acquaintance had noticed her to be not a bad-looking girl. As she and William walked home in the moonlight, Robert having totally forgotten to offer them seats in his carriage, she wondered why William should be so out of temper and should remind her that she had hoped to come home early. She did not remember saying any such thing.

SIX

The informal ball at Teverton, uneventful though it was, justified both Marcia's intuition and Corinna's undeclared intention. From that evening there began a series of changes in the lives of many of the young people present, as if it had been a turning-point. It may have been by coincidence that Mrs Dallow soon lost the habit of referring to her family as 'the children'. Walter, her youngest, who had been dazzled by the uniform of his cousin Henry, announced to her that he intended to enter the army. "Yes," admitted Mrs Dallow with a sigh, "it will I suppose happen, as time passes, that all of you grow up and leave me." She was surprised, rather than regretful, at her own admission; she had never wished to constrain her brood and, were they but in good health, she desired only their happiness, in any part of the world.

Corinna, restless, inquired of her young cousin Silvia all about the fashions and life of Bath, revealing her own longing for a wider world. Robert Pavey, committed to the confines of Fraxted, seemed afflicted after the ball by a gloomier restlessness. His father, watchful still for signs of discontent, misinterpreted Robert's mood, as did Robert himself. Robert himself had not observed that, until now, his life had been undisturbed by serious feeling. Everything he had wanted had come to him; nor had he deeply desired anything; had his symptoms been recognisable to himself, they might have been so to his father, who could then have explained: "You have fallen in love, my boy." As it was, Mr Pavey said to his wife:

"I am afraid Robert is altered lately. His mind is less on his work. He is listless. I wonder if we should make more effort to engage him in such social life as the town offers. He appears in these days to avoid even Teverton. But, speaking of Teverton, I have had it in mind that we ought to invite the Rector there, and his wife, to dinner. Young Collins is a deserving member of the firm and we owe him the courtesy, although I confess I find the effusions of the father tiresome. I can hardly escape him in under half an hour when I meet him in the street."

Mrs Pavey protested that a dinner with the Collinses would not be likely to decrease the dullness of Robert's life, but she agreed that such an invitation should be extended, stipulating only that it might be combined with one of the forthcoming balls at the Assembly Room. "Because, you know, if we are to go out after dinner, we shall not have to put up with them for so long."

"An excellent suggestion. Robert shall find out from young Collins if his family is to come to next month's ball, and if so, we shall arrange a dinner for that evening."

In the Rectory at Teverton, Mr Collins was forming similar if more ambitious designs. "I have decided," he told Mrs Collins, "that, since William and Marcia so much enjoyed the ball at the manor, although I fear that they cannot have expressed their thanks fully or gracefully enough to their kind hosts, indeed, because of that, it is our duty to invite Mr and Mrs Dallow, and their two eldest, to dinner here. I shall write to Mr Dallow immediately, soliciting the honour, and do not doubt that they will flatter us by accepting."

Mrs Collins's method of dealing with her husband was always to agree with him before inserting any objections. She said now: "I am sure they will be delighted to come. I hear, though, that Mr Dallow is to go abroad again very soon. We should not wish to trouble him while he is busy with making preparations for his journey."

"It could not be reckoned a great trouble, for him to come a quarter of a mile to take his dinner. He has not been able to accept any of my invitations in the past, which provides the more reason for me to persist in them. I cannot allow him to feel I am growing less assiduous."

"Perhaps he is not fond of dining out. Although the dinner we should provide would be in no way inferior to his own, yet he may prefer his own family circle, since he is so rarely within it."

"Inferior?" cried Mr Collins. "I trust I am not so negligent of my duty, as not to provide fit entertainment for my own patron, or for anyone else whom I wish to gratify, strain my purse as it might. And Mr Dallow should recollect that he owes a duty to others beyond his own family, neglect those as he may. When he does bestir himself to extend an invitation, be it only to William and Marcia, I am not to be deficient in showing that my own sense of duty is equal to – might I say, exceeds – his. My cloth requires me to provide, besides deference, an example of right conduct."

"I am sure it does, my dear. It is generous of you to wish to show your appreciation of the Dallows' kindess to your family. I wonder if it might not be sufficient, to invite Mr and Mrs Dallow alone. I believe Miss Dallow is engaged to go on a visit to Bath with Miss Webster when she leaves. And Mr George, as we know, is not sociably inclined."

Marcia, who was present, let her needle pause as she glanced up at her mother. Mr Collins was proceeding:

"Then, he must learn to be. In his position, he must look beyond his own pleasures and extend courtesies to those to whom they are due, and especially to those who bear the dignity of my own calling. As for the Miss Dallows, we shall invite one of the others, if the eldest be not available. They are all, I preume, 'out'. Another will do as well."

"Certainly Miss Jane or Miss Philippa would be glad to come. Nor do I believe Mr George to be lacking in politeness. It is merely that he had a riding accident not long ago, and may not be fully recovered."

Marcia's needle paused again and she gazed at her mother in puzzled inquiry. Mrs Collins did not return the look.

"I have had a happy thought," declared Mr Collins after pondering for some moments. For an unguarded instant, Mrs Collins's expression was apprehensive, before with her normal calm she said:

"Yes, my love?"

"I shall invite Mr and Mrs Pavey, together with Mr and Mrs Dallow. That occurs to me as suitable. Mr Pavey is always most amiable to me when I meet him in the street, and I cannot depend on William to repeat often enough his sense of obligation to his master. I shall invite him and his wife here, and endeavour to repair some of that deficiency, besides making up two tables for whist, with William and Marcia. That is my resolution, and I am satisfied that it will please all."

"Yes, my dear, it will. I wish only that the invitation could have come first to us from the Paveys. I am not experienced in these forms, but I feel it would have been more fitting."

Mrs Collins knew well that the absence of any invitation from the Paveys had long been a grievance of her husband's. Reminded now of the Pavey's neglect, Mr

Collins was distracted into deploring that at some length,
and exhausted not only his energy but his verbiage in
describing the ingratitude and disappointments inflicted on
him by the world, to such an ebb that he had to withdraw
to his book room and compose himself by the composition
of a sermon.

It was evident that no invitations were yet to be written.
When the mother and daughter were left alone, Marcia
looked at her mother again as if to speak, but Mrs Collins
said as she snipped her thread:

"If these early frosts are to continue, Jack must bring in
the potatoes from the north field. Remind me to ask him,
Marcia."

"Yes, Mama."

Mrs Collins hoped she had averted the threat of a dinner-
party, for the present. She did not wish to submit many of
the neighbourhood to her husband's society; she was not
herself too fond of it. But nor had she been, even at the stage
of her first meeting him.

Although she had no high opinion of the state of
marriage, she had decided early in life that it was preferable
to the state of spinsterhood. When at the age of twenty-
seven she was still single, she had accepted Mr Collins's
offer of marriage simply for the sake of an establishment.
She knew that his attachment to her must be imaginary,
and that he was in many ways ridiculous, but she had
determined to be a good wife to him and had provided him
with every comfort and attention, excusing or ignoring
everything about him that might have offended her. Her
loyalty to him had extended so far as never to admit his
defects to her friends, or to belittle him in the eyes of his
children. The principle of this latter was right, but she had
been at some risk of sacrificing her children to it. She had
begun to suspect this only since the ball at Teverton, and

only because of an alteration in Marcia that her mother's sympathies had perceived after that evening. Marcia had said little about the ball, but, unable not to confide in her mother, had told her of George Dallow's riding accident, which had taken place two days ago, and from which George was fully recovered. Mrs Collins and Marcia knew this, so it was her mother's suggestion that he might not be recovered which had puzzled Marcia. It was as yet beyond Marcia to imagine that her mother might wish to obstruct her father's social enterprises.

The riding accident, which Marcia had witnessed, still occupied her mind to the exclusion of any speculation on her parents' convivial plans.

Two days before, Marcia had been alone in the lane above the Rectory, gathering sprays of autumn leaves, when George Dallow came cantering down on his roan mare. There had been, as Mrs Collins had remarked, some frosts and under a drift of leaves in the lane was hidden a patch of ice. The mare slipped on this, striking her fore hoof on a stone, falling to her knees and throwing George violently from the saddle. He hit his head against the bole of a tree and lay white-faced and insensible.

Marcia flung down her leaves and ran to kneel beside him, calling his name and, amid her terror, conscious of a strange, womanly tenderness rising in herself as she gazed down at him. George, resilient as any Dallow, opened his eyes and gazed back at her saying:

"Lord, what a smash. Where is the mare?"

The mare was waiting nearby and George had to be satisfied that she had not broken her knees before he would pay any attention to his own injuries. These, he insisted, were negligible.

"But you must come into the Rectory," cried Marcia, "and we shall send for Dr Ingle. Or at the least," as he protested, "you must rest yourself, and take a glass of wine —"

"I assure you, I am in no need of any assistance. I shall walk the mare to the foot of the lane, to be sure that she is not lamed, and by then, my head will have stopped swimming, and I shall mount." This he did, Marcia accompanying him. Before leaping to the saddle he took her hands and said in friendly warmth: "You are a good girl and I am deuced — That is, very grateful to you." Off he cantered, apparently restored and cheerful. Marcia went home more in need of restoratives than he, to tell her mother of the adventure. Mrs Collins, administering wine and water, divined her daughter's feelings, and Marcia, in her shaken condition, was not reticent of them.

"He said I was a good girl, but then, he is so easy and kind, he would say that to anyone. Indeed, I did nothing to help him. And when he danced with me, twice, at their house, it was because there was no other partner available, I dare say. I shall make nothing of it. But do you not think, Mama, he is splendid? He is so fine-looking and so brave. When he lay there in the lane, and I feared he was killed, I was more frightened than I have ever been in my life. I suppose I shall not see him again, or not for many weeks, but I wish I could be sure that he is truly not hurt. Do not collisions of the head sometimes show their effects only afterwards?"

Mrs Collins attempted to reassure her as to the superhuman thickness of George Dallow's skull, and soon Marcia regained her composure, setting aside the glass:

"Thank you, the wine has made me quite myself again. Pay no attention, Mama, to the nonsense I talked. It was merely that I had had a shock. Now I shall go and gather some more leaves, and then write the letter I promised to my aunt Maria."

When William returned from his day's work in Fraxted he said: "Marcia, Mr Robert says I am to tell you that Mr George told him at midday that he and his mare are in perfect health. I do not know what to make of the message, but I repeat it as given."

William may have made nothing of the message, but Mrs Collins saw that it gave her daughter great satisfaction. She pitied and admired Marcia, while not opening again between them the topic of George Dallow. She could observe in Marcia the conflict between natural good sense and a young girl's newly awakened heart. Mrs Collins pitied her daughter in that this first attraction had to be towards a young man so far beyond her reach, but admired her in that Marcia was making a determined effort to subdue her feelings. She trusted Marcia to govern herself, but did not wish to submit her yet to such an ordeal as a dinner-party in George Dallow's presence. Too tactful to explain this, Mrs Collins did all she could to exempt George from a visit to the Rectory, and then continued to sew and speak of potatoes.

Mrs Collins, with her own life history in mind, had intended from the first that Marcia should marry young and marry well. She did not mean that there should be great wealth or love in the union; affection and respectability were sufficient. She hoped however, as mothers will, that her daughter should be happier than she herself had been. Not designing, she was equally not neglectful of possibilities. When Marcia was born Mrs Collins had begun to consider them and had felt that Walter Dallow might be suitable as a husband in due time. The younger son, and about two years older than Marcia, and probably destined for orders and some family living of value comparable to Teverton's, he should be in every way eligible. Time revealed, however, that Walter was an unlikely candidate for the clerical profession, nor did the Dallow temperament accord with Marcia's.

When Marcia was old enough to be taken into company Mrs Collins assessed more immediately the respectable young men of the district without selecting any one. That no young man selected Marcia did not trouble her mother; she knew Marcia's worth and, besides, found her too valuable a companion to wish soon to part with her. Only recently, since the ball at Teverton, had Mrs Collins resumed her thought on the subject of husband-seeking. She must compel herself to give up Marcia; Marcia had shown herself susceptible to male attraction and Marcia now needed some antidote to George Dallow. Upon reflection, Mrs Collins concluded that Robert Pavey qualified most highly as candidate for Marcia's hand. She formed hopes, but no plans, on this account and spoke of it to no one.

SEVEN

Sociability was in the air. The success of his little hall had inspired Mr Dallow to pursue the hospitable initiative and he too decided to give a dinner-party. "It is a pity the Bewleys will not be here before I leave, but there will be enough without them. The Paveys, I thought we might have. John Pavey is annoyed with me because I will not closet myself with him over all those deeds and trusts *et cetera*, but as it is, I shall not have time to complete my tabulation of Roman potsherds before I go. Is there anyone else to whom we owe a dinner, Mrs Dallow? I lose touch."

"Do you think," his wife suggested, "we should ask the Collinses?"

The groan that arose, as of one voice, from the assembled family would have provided an excellent opportunity of mortification for its Rector. Mrs Dallow said in apology: "They are, you see, for ever asking us."

"That may be, but we have never accepted," Corinna pointed out.

"No; so we can be said to owe them nothing," said Mr Dallow. "Is there anyone, I wonder, whom Silvia would like to meet?" He was showing much favour to his pretty little cousin.

"Thank you, but there is no one I know of, sir. I am very happy to be among the family. That is company enough."

Silvia said this with all sincerity and with some relief. She could, now, scarcely remember why she had been so much afraid when she visited Teverton as a child, so pleasant was she finding her present stay. The sunny autumn weather had continued and the woods and grounds of the manor could conceal no terrors. The Hall too was quieter, and her cousins more gently attentive to her. No one dared her to climb the tall pear tree, or to go and see whether the butler had hanged himself in the pantry. She could go upstairs to bed without the apprehension of a sheeted figure's hurtling from a cupboard, horribly shrieking, to blow out her candle. Had this occurred, Silvia felt she might have borne it with only momentary alarm. She shrank more from the recollection of herself as she must have been, a white-faced little coward, impeding her cousins' pleasures, continually to be waited for and searched for. She wondered that they could be so kind to her now, when they must then have despised her. She was glad that she had extended her visit, and did not remember begging Henry to take her away again directly after the ball, when the invitation was first in prospect. Walter, and Philippa, sometimes teased her a little, and George was always absent about his sporting concerns, but Corinna and Jane treated her as amiably as if she were in no way inferior to them. Indeed, they deferred to her as to a visitor from a wider world, asking her in tireless detail about Bath and her life there.

"I dare say we should find the balls there much too fashionable for us," Jane said as they walked in the gardens. "Are they not very grand?"

"No, I think not. Not, in comparison with what Henry tells me of London. He has many friends there. Bath is busy only during its season."

"Do you go often to balls?"

"No, not often. When Henry takes me, I attend them."

"I fancied you must want to go. I know I should. Does not Mrs Forbes feel obliged to take you into society? Does she not hope to find you a husband?"

"She has not told me so," said Silvia laughing. "But when you come to visit us, I am sure she will do her best to find one for you."

"She would need to," said Corinna laughing too. "We should know no one there. Does she have a wide acquaintance?"

"She has many friends, yes. But when one attends a ball in Bath, the master of ceremonies can perform introductions if necessary. I confess, although I enjoy dancing, I do not care for the crowds when Bath is full. I should prefer to live in the country, rather than in a town."

"Whereas I," cried Corinna, "would give anything to live in a town, among crowds and shops and people. Shopping would be the best of it. I adore good shops. It is no wonder that my father says we are all spendthrifts, since we have so little chance to visit anywhere other than Thompson's in Fraxted, that when we do, we go wild. Nor do I know how he dare accuse us, because he is a spendthrift himself over his old Roman coins and scraps of dirty Egyptian stone – Nay, Silvia, do not look at me with such reproach. I am not speaking disrespectfully of him. It is only what he says about himself."

"I meant no reproof," Silvia protested, "as I am sure you meant no disrespect."

"Confess it, however," went on Corinna. "You do find our manners wild altogether, after what you have been used to at home."

"No, I do not. I admire you, and wish I had your beauty and vitality, and courage in putting forward my opinions."

"Do not be over-modest. You know that you are very pretty. Everyone says so. And, by the way, I do not know why I refer to Bath as your home. Teverton is supposed to be your home, and if you would like to live in the country, I wish you would feel free to make it so. We should all be happy to have you."

Silvia could not doubt this. Mr and Mrs Dallow made her welcome as if they were retrieving a daughter, Mrs Dallow exhibiting affection in her particular fashion:

"I never wished it, as you know," she told Silvia when they were alone, "that you should go away from us, and I did not expect to see you back, each time you left us after one of your visits; how thankful I am that you have been spared to us, in the relaxing air of such a place as Bath. I am astonished that you have survived it, and being so much indoors, as you must have been. I have worried continually that not enough care was being given to your health. It is marvellous to me that you look as well as you do. There is colour even in your fingernails, and the texture of your hair – Allow me to touch it, my dear? – Yes, the texture of your hair is satisfactory. I have received a pamphlet, new out from London, explaining that the texture of hair is a sure indication of general health. It must not be too soft, nor cling to the fingers, nor lie close. I am a little troubled about Jane's. In case your lungs are in any danger, I will prepare you a decoction of cranesbill root seethed in milk, an old specific, but revived again by a clever doctor from Devonshire, who has written a booklet – I shall lend it to you, and you may convince yourself. I hope you will be as faithful as the others, in walking at a fast pace to the orchard gates and back, every morning before breakfast."

Silvia had been obedient in the morning walk, which in the current weather was no hardship, and was ready to swallow the decoction of cranesbill, out of affection for Mrs Dallow, whom she thanked for all her kindness.

"Think nothing of that, my dear child; who should have

your interests closer at heart, than your own relations? I
will believe Mrs Forbes is a very good sort of person, and
she has taken better care of you than I expected, but she
cannot undertake the responsibility of establishing you in
life. I am afraid she may introduce you into the wrong
society in Bath, where every sort of undesirable person may
forgather, and allow you to be caught by some young man
whom we should think unsuitable."

"I do not wish to marry," said Silvia with a colour rising
in her face.

"Well, not yet, perhaps. But nor can Mrs Forbes keep
you with her for the rest of your life."

"She is very dear to me," Silvia said, her eyes filling.

"She has been very good to you, and it shows your sweet
nature that you are fond of her. But who is she, after all?
Her husband, I hear, was some sort of naval man, who
made so little provision for her, that when he died, she had
to take a position as paid companion to your Aunt Mallory.
Who is her own family, that no one supported her? Well,
my dear, do not look so sad. Nothing shall be decided in a
hurry. Bear it in mind that your true friends are here, and
be happy with us. Take the air as much as you can. I wish
you would ask George to find you a quiet horse to ride. He
would be so glad to help and instruct you."

Silvia had perhaps outgrown her fear of her cousin
George, but not her fear of horses. After this interview she
went first to her room, to shed some tears of homesickness
and regret for Mrs Forbes, and then recovering her spirits
went to find occupation that would keep her too busy to
have leisure for George and his horse, should he approach
with any such threat. He did not, and Silvia helped Jane to
brush and comb a litter of puppies, which supplied
amusement for the rest of the morning, and enabled Silvia
to forget her homesickness; or, as Corinna would have had

it, her Bath-sickness.

Bath was, nevertheless, Silvia's home and Mrs Forbes was to her all that a mother could have been. Riding, or strenuous exercise, may not have had a great part in Mrs Forbes's direction of Silvia, but she had bestowed much care on her education, engaging masters for music and painting, yet sending her to school, largely in order to help Silvia overcome her shyness. Silvia had been well suited by this studious and tranquil life, not caring to go into company except when required by her brother Henry, giving no serious thought to her future. Her early timidity may have caused her to set a small value on herself; she did not believe Corinna, who said that 'everyone' said she was pretty; she had never inquired about the extent of her fortune and so had no idea what Mrs Dallow was hinting at, when she spoke of Silvia's being 'caught' by some unworthy suitor. All that had troubled her, in Mrs Dallow's conversation, was the implied criticism of Mrs Forbes, and that, in playing with the puppies, she presently forgot.

"Do you hear," asked Jane as she at last settled the last puppy to sleep in its basket, "that terrible noise Philippa is making?"

"Is it Philippa who is playing the pianoforte?"

"If so one could call it, yes. I fancy Papa has told her to practise, in case she is asked to play tomorrow evening. Come, Silvia, you must help her. Soon she will work herself into a rage, and take that out on the poor instrument – with a meat-cleaver, from the sound of it."

Both girls went to Philippa's rescue. Jane had been right: The dinner-party was to be held tomorrow and Mr Dallow had reminded his daughters that music might be called for. Corinna and Jane could sing a duet, but Philippa, as she recounted in exasperation to Silvia, could play but one piece upon the pianoforte, and that she had neglected for so long that she had forgotten how to play it.

"But in any event," she said, "I hope I shall not be needed. You must play your longest piece, Silvia, and besides, they will surely ask you twice, since you are the newcomer. Then when Corinna and Jane have sung, my efforts will not be required."

"Shall I be asked to play?" said Silvia in some alarm. "If so, I must practise as well."

"Oh, no, you do not need to practise, you play so well. Show me, Silvia, how I should perform this insipid Rondo in G. You will put me to shame, but you could help me with the fingering; I have it all wrong."

Silvia, disclaiming, was nevertheless able to give Philippa some advice on the execution of the piece, which Philippa received willingly. She was no musician and remarked as she slammed shut the lid of the pianoforte:

"Well, if my father wishes his dinner-party to be a failure, he is making provision for it. I shall not play if I can help it. Silvia, do not be nervous of your own performance; playing such as yours will more than compensate for mine. In any case, no one musical will be here, excepting Mrs Ingle, and she never stops talking, so will not listen."

Mrs Ingle was the wife of Dr Ingle, the leading medical practitioner in Fraxted. Relations between the good doctor and Mrs Dallow were cool, for Dr Ingle had not Mrs Dallow's reliance on new pamphlets out of London. Nor, in all circumstances, had Mr Dallow; so he persisted in retaining the doctor's friendship, in order that his family might have orthodox medical aid at hand in any crisis. Dr Ingle dined happily at the manor while its master was at home, as long as the topic of medicine was avoided.

On this occasion, besides the Ingles, Mr Dallow had invited the Paveys and Robert, two old friends Mr and Mrs Downing, and Mr Prebble, an antiquarian acquaintance of

his own; the lamps of whose carriages were observed by Mr
Collins from the window of his book-room, as they swept up
the lane to the Hall and duly returned. As dinner was about
to be announced, there also arrived Bernard Phillips, the
friend of George; it appeared that Corinna, meeting him
during a ride, had invited him, but forgotten to mention it
at home. Another place was quickly set, however, and the
food was sufficient. After this momentary confusion, the
evening ran smoothly. The dinner was lavish, without being
spendthrift enough to trouble Mr Pavey; everyone looked
well; Bernard Phillips was not allowed to guess that he was
unexpected. He was a personable, if not brilliant, young
man whose estate marched with the Dallows'. Since his
father's early death Bernard had devoted himself to the
estate's management. Three years ago he had proposed
marriage to Corinna, who had laughed at him. It was to his
credit that Bernard had survived that indignity and
remained a family friend. Corinna had laughed at the idea
of herself as marriageable, rather than at Bernard, who was
still in love with her but would not dare admit it to her
again. This evening he admired her as deeply as ever, or
indeed more so; he sensed a new spirit in her, which
rendered her more handsome and graceful; he could not
imagine that he had aspired to her.

In rather similar case was Robert Pavey, on beholding
Miss Webster again. He had been far from any idea of
aspiring to her; but, seeing her anew, he felt her to be more
of a vision than a reality. His memory of her had been
inadequate. As he sat opposite to her at the dinner-table he
had the exquisite sensation of a waking dream. It was
fortunate that he was not required to speak to her; to speak
to anyone, at present, would have been impossible. In fact,
speech was rendered impossible by his having Mrs Ingle by
his side, in whose proximity no one else's speech stood a

chance. Across the table, Miss Webster's attention was monopolised by Mr Prebble the antiquarian, who was describing to her the ruined temples of Persia. An observer would have supposed Mr Prebble's disquisition to be more interesting than Mrs Ingle's, for while Miss Webster's eyes turned constantly to him, Robert's were fixed in an absent gaze over the table towards her. He may have been excused for it, since the ruined temples of Persia, or almost any subject, must have held more edification than Mrs Ingle's trivial account of her own doings. Like most inveterate talkers, she did not pause to wonder whether anyone listened to her; and listening was not easy, since she had another not uncommon habit of the garrulous: that of unreeling her stories backwards, so that their point receded until it was lost sight of. In this instance she had begun by promising to tell Robert of a most astonishing experience that had befallen her during a recent carriage drive to Malston Woods, whither she had wished to take her sister, who had been on a visit to her, from London, where she had latterly suffered an accident, not of a grave nature, for she had merely slipped on the step of her house and broken a bone of her ankle, but for some while walking had been impossible and so she had been conveyed to Fraxted for company and cosseting, which she had appreciated, for she lived alone in London since the sad death of her husband, some seven years ago, from an affliction of the heart, at the age of only forty years, a severe shock to them all, for he had been a vigorous man, and indeed had been used to walk to his business in the City every day, from his house in Finsbury, for the exercise, and as a young man had excelled at all sports, as had his whole family, who had come to England from Jamaica, where they possessed plantations, which had been totally demolished by a tropical storm, so that Mrs Ingle's brother-in-law had been as a young man

virtually penniless and had built up his business from
nothing ...

"... But by great industry, and with ability, he
established himself in a very good way, though not before
he had set by enough to support his mother, for his father
soon died, disappointed after his ruin, and what is more, he
took care of his two younger sisters, one of whom soon
married a barrister, while the other, who was delicate,
having I believe taken some fever as a small child in those
tropic regions, did not regain strength, for which my
brother-in-law always blamed a native nurse they had as
children, who treated her little charges after a primitive
fashion as of course, the natives will, if they are not taught
any better, and I am afraid the parents may have been at
fault, for the mother, as I understand, was given over to
gaieties and neglectful of her family, being of French
extraction, though of good family, indeed I am told her
grandfather had been a Marquis ..."

By the end of the dinner, the ancestry of Mrs Ingle's
brother-in-law's mother's grandfather bid fair to pre-date
the Persian ruins, and Malston Woods were still not
reached. Robert, entering the drawing-room with the other
gentlemen, saw that Miss Webster was helping Corinna to
pour coffee at a side table. Corinna, unwitting, fulfilled his
desire by calling him to them.

"Robert, you must commiserate with Silvia, and she with
you. You both had a dull dinner of it, and I am sorry. You
were each seated beside a relentless monologuist and had
no respite."

Robert and Silvia were enabled to exchange sympathetic
smiles. "I found what Mr Prebble had to say very
interesting" Silvia said. "But I am too ignorant to
understand or remember much of it."

"Oh, Silvia, you must not be always belittling yourself.

You are not ignorant, compared with me, and you know it." Silvia blushed slightly under this rallying tone and Robert longed to defend her. "What was old Prebble boring you with? I should not even have troubled myself to listen," Corinna was pursuing.

"He told me," said Silvia, hesitant, "that Mesopotamia is thought by some to be the cradle of the oldest civilisation in the world."

"There, you see. At the next party you attend, you may announce that, and be thought clever."

"I do not wish to be thought clever, Corinna."

"No, you wish to be thought nothing. But was she not clever, Robert, to listen to Mr Prebble as she did?"

"Miss Webster had a more profitable dinner than I," Robert said. "I failed to understand what Mrs Ingle was speaking of at all."

They all laughed, and very beautiful it made Miss Webster in Robert's eyes. Her humour was as charming to him as her modesty. Corinna moved away, bidding Walter pass coffee to the other guests, and Robert cast about for any remark that could detain Miss Webster. He could think of nothing. To his delight, she addressed him:

"You were wrong, Mr Pavey, in saying that I did not remember you, when we met at the ball here. How could I forget the day when the stream was flooded, and the others ran over the stepping-stones under the water, and left me, but you came back and carried me across?"

The tribute was undeserved. Robert did, now, seem to remember such an incident; but the impulse that had made him turn back and collect the little cousin had been of impatience rather than of pity. Praise unmerited, however, can have the greater value, in coming as sheer gift, and his inner glow of gratification was the brighter. He wished only that he might have the opportunity of carrying her over a thousand more flooded streams, and in his thankfulness almost said so. It was perhaps fortunate that, at that moment, Jane called:

"Silvia, Papa is asking you to play for us!"

Thereafter, music commanded the party. Silvia went obediently to the pianoforte, without real nervousness, for Mrs Forbes had taught her to place the music before the listeners, and so to absorb herself in that and forget her shyness. She chose a sonata long enough, she hoped, to please Philippa without tiring the others, and before she was halfway through the slow movement Mrs Ingle was in full anecdote: "... But I did not buy it, because on the day before I had been in another shop for ribbon, which I needed for trimming a bonnet, which had been spoilt when I was caught in the rain one day, on my way to called on Mrs Peters, for I had heard her son was expected home from Edinburgh, where he has been, you know, these several years, studying to be a doctor, although at first they intended him for the navy, because two of his uncles ..." Meanwhile Mrs Dallow, having placed herself within earshot of Dr Ingle, was telling Mrs Downing of the excellence of her family's health; a cat had scratched Philippa's finger last week, but the wound had healed after only one application of salve, which indicated the fine condition of her daughter's blood. Philippa, also overhearing that, regretted the salve; she might otherwise have pleaded infirmity and let her damaged finger exempt her from the Rondo in G.

As she had hoped, her performance was not in the event called for. Such of the company as listened to the music, and in particular Robert, begged Silvia to favour them with another piece. After a shorter one, she begged in turn to be allowed to give way to Corinna and Jane, who sang their duet. "Let us get it over with," was Corinna's concession.

"We have sung this same song since we were in the schoolroom, and no one can want to hear it again." Their voices, if not highly trained, were fresh and sweet, and of this song Mr Dallow himself never grew tired. "I am fond of the old-fashioned airs," he said. "Let us hear some more."

"Let Silvia sing," cried Jane. "She sings as well as she plays."

Silvia demurred, but to please Mr Dallow she drew on her memory for a simple folk song, finding no songs that she had studied among the scanty collection of books by the pianoforte. Corinna and Jane joined with her in the last stanza.

"Bravo!" applauded Mr Dallow. "Why, we have the makings of a choir here. George, I have heard you and Walter shouting that song about the house often enough as children. Robert, you must know it too. Shall we hear you all together?"

George, who had been apparently in low spirits all evening, shook his head. Walter said: "I cannot sing, sir, but Robert can, I know. He told us that he and some friends formed a glee club at Oxford. Have we no book with that song in? If Robert would take the tenor part, I would attempt to growl out the bass." There followed more rummagings through books, and essays at songs that no one thoroughly knew, until there was more merriment than music on that side of the room, and Mrs Ingle was distracted from her current narrative:

"What are you all laughing about?" she asked, rising from her sofa and crossing the room. "Were you trying to render that song in four parts? You had the harmony false, Corinna. Let me show you." And, pausing only to describe to them when she had last, previously, and first heard the song, she played it through, drilling the impromptu choir into fair order. She was a competent musician and would have had them progress to a more difficult song, but the mood of the party denied this.

"No, let us sing something easy and jolly," said Walter. "Robert, what of the glees that you sang with your friends?"

"I do not think they would be suitable to mixed company."

"Robert, I am surprised at you," said Corinna in mock solemnity.

Mrs Ingle declared: "What young men sing together over their wine, and what they sing with ladies in the drawing-room, are distinct types of music and must be allowed for."

"That is a broad-minded attitude, Mrs Ingle," cried the pert Walter. "And pray how do you come to be conversant with young men's drinking-songs?"

He ran the risk of a lengthy backward explanation, but Mrs Ingle said merely: "I do not say that I am. Robert —" her mind being still upon music, "I have at home a volume of old Irish songs, and one of Scotch, that I will lend to you. I will leave them with the servant, and you may call at our house for them at any time, and bring them up here to try over with Miss Webster. Your two voices blend well."

Robert felt himself in great good luck, to have a pretext for coming again to the manor, and to see Miss Webster, thus presented to him unsolicited. As Miss Webster appeared not displeased by the offer, he thanked Mrs Ingle warmly and then in his exhilaration proposed: "Walter, shall you and I challenge the ladies in 'One man shall mow my meadow', letting them be the ewes and lambs while we are the rams, and we shall see who makes the more mistakes in the counting?" The young Dallows fell in readily with this absurd suggestion, fatal to the evening's formality. The party became worthy of the Dallows at their noisiest, goodwill increasing until even Mr Prebble, when twenty-seven men were on the point of mowing the meadow, mentioned with real dismay that he must soon leave, as he had an early journey on the morrow.

"A most amusing evening, was it not, Robert?" said Mrs Ingle to him as he closed the instrument for her.

"One of the happiest of my life," Robert replied; then, recollecting himself: "Yes, most enjoyable. The Dallows, of course, are the best of hosts; their high spirits are infectious."

"So they are; but I wonder why George is so grave tonight?"

"No doubt his best horse has lost a race. I shall be glad to come for your song-books, Mrs Ingle, and should appreciate the honour of calling on yourself, if I may." He had not known that Mrs Ingle could be so genial; at this moment, his benevolence embraced humankind.

"I hope we shall meet again soon, Robert. You are becoming quite a gallant gentleman. You were always, I remember, somewhat passive as a little boy. Or it may have been, that these exuberant Dallows kept you in their shade. You appear now more equal to them."

"Indeed I hope I am," said Robert, taken aback by her forthrightness. "And I hope we shall meet soon, Mrs Ingle, perhaps at my parents' house. Though I am afraid," he remembered, "that the next excitement planned there, is to have the Collinses to dinner. That party will not compare with this. I cannot imagine the Collinses joining in foolish songs."

"No more can I." Outspoken still, Mrs Ingle said: "I am sorry for Mrs Collins. She is a good-humoured, clever woman, and how she came to marry such a husband as hers, I cannot imagine."

Mrs Dallow overheard this. "I agree with you. I have nothing against Mrs Collins. She does good work in the parish, and her children have, from their looks, been brought up in fair enough health."

"Yes, that is so. I am sure Dr Ingle has been as rarely at that Rectory, as at any house in the district. Excepting yours, ma'am, of course," Mrs Ingle could not resist adding; but Mrs Dallow took that as a compliment.

EIGHT

Mrs Collins might have been glad to know that she had the sympathy of some of the ladies of the neighbourhood, yet a proper pride in her would have rejected it. In her heart she did not believe that even her friends had forgiven her for her marriage. Deeper in her heart, she had not perhaps forgiven herself, but she did not examine deeply what was past remedy. She had made a choice, in full awareness, and if a slight reserve lingered between her and those who were equally aware of her motives, all Mrs Collins could do was to make the best of her circumstances and admit no doubts or regrets. Any misfortune she suffered, she would admit that she had brought upon herself.

This admission Mr Collins, for his part, would never entertain. It was true that the early promise of his life had been blighted through no omission of his own. The falling in love of one man, and the longevity of another, were accidents whose effects on Mr Collins no one could maliciously have planned. By an accident of nature, perhaps, Mr Collins was not endowed with his wife's gifts of contentment and resignation. Far from counting his blessings, he discounted them, in his constant lamentation that they were no greater. To his obsequiousness and complacency, Mrs Collins had become inured. His increasing plaintiveness was an added trial, especially as

she could see no valid reason for pitying him, and she was
rendered unhappy as throughout their marriage she had
not hitherto been.

It was not a happy time for anyone at the Rectory.
Marcia put a brave, but not convincingly cheerful, face
upon her private feelings, and her mother respected her
reticence; but they were less close. William was, to use his
father's word, sullen. No one could wring a word from him.
It was not only that he was tongue-tied; some inner gloom
was to be inferred; not only could he not, but he would not,
speak, except to tell his mother or Marcia, when they
persuaded him to confide in them, that there was nothing
amiss.

William meant that simply and sincerely. 'Nothing' was
what he seemed nowadays to suffer from. A sense of his own
nonentity had descended upon him, on the evening of the
ball at Teverton, and he could conceive of no relief. He had
been glad for Marcia that she had enjoyed the ball and had
danced with Mr George; but for himself, the occasion had
been as dull as he had rendered it, by his own stupidity. Mr
Robert had forgotten to bring him and Marcia home,
which William had not taken offence at; but, since that
evening, Mr Robert had been aloof in the office, offering
Fitz no amusing stories, dawdling in an abstracted fashion
over his own work; William could not imagine how he had
lost Mr Robert's friendship, but assumed that he deserved
to. He was upon the verge of taking refuge in despondency.

"I observe," said Mr Collins, coming in from his book-
room, "that Mr Dallow has departed. The carriage has
passed, with all his trunks. One deduces that he will again
be abroad for an extended period. He has vouchsafed me no
word, even of farewell. Had I been in any way remiss in my
duty, as clergyman or neighbour, I should be disposed
humbly to submit to such neglect. But my conscience is

clear, which renders my tribulation the sorer. I have suffered too long under what must in all charity be termed the incivility of such a patron, and am at the end of my forbearance." What he could do about this, apart from continuing to say so, he did not surmise. "I declare that I am greatly to be pitied," he told his family, before withdrawing again to his book-room. He was to be pitied; but in being the first to point this out he, according to the perversity of human nature, forfeited pity.

When, two days later, an invitation to dinner at the manor was delivered, Mr Collins was not disposed to be gratified by it.

"I must protest that any invitation so long delayed loses its value. And, to wait in this instance until Mr Dallow himself is gone! Am I to be bidden to Teverton Hall only when there is a paucity of society? Aware as I am of the obligation of Christian forgiveness, right principle tempts me to refuse this invitation. It is a blow upon the face."

Avoiding the scriptural injunction to those thus smitten, Mrs Collins said: "I am surprised that Mrs Dallow should be so discourteous."

"There is no discourtesy in an invitation. I complain only of the manner and timing of it. I am not to be tricked into the equivalent discourtesy of a refusal."

"I am glad to hear you say so, my love. Your generosity can exceed the Dallows' incivility. Mrs Dallow must be well aware that the gesture is overdue."

Mrs Dallow was. It was only when she heard that the Paveys were to invite the Collinses to dine, that she made up her mind that she must at last do so. In the commotion of packing and departure Mrs Dallow had forgotten again about the Collineses, but as soon as she was at leisure she had issued the invitation, hoping to forestall the Paveys, whose invitation as far as she knew had not been sent. She remarked to Philippa: "It is strange that it comes about, when your father is home and we arrange to do so much entertaining, yet we omit to invite those to whom we have a prior obligation."

Philippa answered: "If by 'obligation' you mean the Collinses, I am not surprised that you happen to omit them."

"Now, Philippa, do not be so unfriendly. The Rector and his family have lived almost at our doorstep for all your lifetime, and you have made no attempt to know them."

Philippa might with justice have returned that reproof, but she said only, with indifference: "That does not surprise me to recall, either."

Mrs Collins knew that the invitation should be, and ultimately would be, accepted. She resigned herself to the ordeal of going with her husband into company, little expecting that she would be required to do so twice.

Mr Collins deliberated earnestly before replying to Mrs Dallow. "It may be my duty to show an example of magnanimity. I wish I could know of whom the party is to be composed. No doubt the Paveys are expected. In that case, would my obligation be increased? William, you must ask Mr Robert whether the Paveys are to go, and if so, who else. You must phrase the question delicately, and please see to it that you express yourself graciously and do not sound inquisitive."

William, perforce undertaking the commission, phrased the question: "Mr Robert, are you dining with the Dallows next Thursday?" and received the equally indelicate answer: "No; we are engaged to go to the Brownes." Whereat both young men resumed their work. But soon after, Robert, reminded, made occasion to go upstairs and remind his mother in turn that the Collinses were to be invited to dine before the public ball. "Fitz mentioned something about dining," he told her, "and I wondered whether he and his family had been invited to us; he has not spoken of it."

"Oh, heavens, I had forgotten!" exclaimed Mrs Pavey. "I am so thankful to you, Robert. Please bring me my writing-desk and I will see to it at once – and please do not tell your father I had forgotten."

So it came about that the Collinses received both overdue invitations in rapid sequence. Between his sense of insult and his sense of his own dignity, Mr Collins's deliberations became confused, and he wrote to accept both invitations in phrases of the most felicitous gratitude, as his wife had known that he all along intended.

The Collinses had all along intended also to go to the public ball. Once or twice during each winter they did so, and the first of the season would be a full one, and worth attending. Mr Collins liked to display his family on occasion, so long as he himself were present to cover up the deficiency of William's manners and to describe Marcia's virtues to any parents to whose respectable sons he could recommend her. He would explain that it was upon his children's account that he himself went to the balls, although balls, if properly conducted, were not below the ecclesiastical estimation. Mrs Collins hoped at this moment that the ball would relieve Marcia's spirits and that a little social exertion would rouse William too from his depression of mind. Of the prior gathering at the Hall, she had no such expectation, the more so since she had heard in the village that Miss Webster was gone back to Bath, taking Miss Dallow and Miss Jane with her on a visit, and that Mr George had escorted them thither. The party would be small; but, she consoled herself, there would be the fewer witnesses of Mr Collins's extravagances of appreciation.

Hearing of the departure of the majority of the Dallow

family before his reception among them, Mr Collins began to repent of his acceptance of his invitation, but he could not revoke it, and indeed, with the two dinners in prospect, he yielded to his own more cheerful urges and began to anticipate pleasure, exhorting his wife to prepare his linen to total perfection and his children to conduct themselves as would be suitable to each occasion.

"Upon my word, Marcia, you are indeed launched now into the world of fashion, and are living a delightful life," he informed his daughter. "But you must not let it turn your head. Another new gown will not be necessary. Make yourself as neat as possible, and be as modest in your bearing as befits a young girl, bearing in mind always that you are the daughter of the Rectory and hence worthy of some of the respect that reflects from myself. Smile agreeably, and speak only when you are addressed."

This latter, Marcia was herself resolved upon. As Mr George was from home, she looked forward without alarm to the evening at the Hall, for she liked Mrs Dallow and was at ease with the unaffected affability of the youngest Dallows. Her alarm was the greater, when the Collinses entered the drawing-room at Teverton to see Mr George standing before the hearth. The only other guest, Bernard Phillips, had arrived ahead of the Collinses, and to him George was explaining:

"... Walter was so eager to go, because he had formed some splendid picture of the pleasures of Bath – whence, I do not know – and he would not be withheld. Whereas I have so much business on hand here, with the hunting season upon us, and so on, that I yielded to him –"

He broke off to greet the newcomers, while Mrs Dallow, from the sofa where she sat with Philippa, took up George's explanation, adding that although she feared the sultry air of Bath, Walter might there find some treatment, which

Silvia had spoken of as successful with a friend of Mrs Forbes's, to prevent his cough from recurring in the winter. George, with a smile at Marcia, said:

"Aye – Walter developed an amazing horrid cough as soon as my mother mentioned that. But I am sure Bath will alleviate it."

Marcia's composure was now equal to her giving the smile that was sufficient reply. She had no need of words, because Mr Collins was already thanking Mrs Dallow for her invitation, praising the proportions of the room and the style of its furnishings, the evident good health of her son and daughter, and repeating on behalf of his family their heartfelt sense of the honour bestowed upon them in being received into so magnificent an abode.

"There is nothing magnificent about it," Mrs Dallow at last interrupted, in her straightforward manner. To Mrs Collins she added: "It is but a small family dinner, I am afraid, but a small party can be sometimes comfortable. It is more intimate, and one has more opportunity of speaking to each one."

"My dear lady," took up Mr Collins, "I concur entirely with your sentiments. Nothing is more pleasant than an intimate gathering, in which conversation is general, to the exclusion of none, and all may share in the exchange of elevated thoughts that are all too often not permitted by the tumult, and in some cases the frivolity, of a large party, although I certainly intend no reference, as I know you will believe, to any hospitality which you yourself might be gracious enough to extend, and of which I can furnish the instance of the ball to which you were kind enough to invite my own son and daughter not long ago, and of which they have spoken on every succeeding day with unbounded admiration and gratitude, so conscious were they of the honour accorded to them. And no less will they humbly appreciate such an evening as this, when, to borrow you own apt word, the atmosphere is more intimate, and each one has the privilege of communicating and contributing to the general harmoniousness." In this fashion denying all present the privilege he extolled, Mr Collins continued as far as the dining-room his rhapsodies of admiration for the table, the china and the portraits on the walls.

Mrs Collins preserved her usual calm, and as soon as her husband's mouth was stopped by a mouthful of food, which he must imbibe in order to enable him to praise it, she turned to Mrs Dallow with a question about an old woman who lay ill in a cottage above the woods, and whose welfare was the concern of both parish and manor. In the course of their charitable work, these two ladies frequently encountered each other, Mrs Dallow having energy to spare to cherish the health of her tenants as well as of her family. She replied at some length, appending her opinions on the diet of the old woman's grandchildren. George interposed: "Oh, come Mama, you know old Sykes takes rabbits enough to supply meat for any number of children!" but, apart from the one insertion, everyone else was silent. Marcia's eyes were lowered, because she was placed opposite Mr George at the table. William too kept his gaze on his plate, feeling called upon for no contribution. When Mr Collins resumed his discourse, declaring that soup of such exquisite flavour had never before passed his lips, and he must compliment Mrs Dallow and her cook, George said:

"I must be included in your congratulations, sir, since it was I who shot the hares that went into the soup."

"Indeed, sir, your marksmanship is much to be praised, and I would not in any way seem to deny you your just tribute of compliment. I trust you feel no slight or omission was intended. Nothing could be further from my intention."

Marcia did not observe the glances that passed among George, Philippa and Bernard, indicative of barely withheld mirth. It occurred to her only that Mr George was in gay spirits this evening, in comparison with his mood on the evening of the ball. The glances of the young trio were observed by Mrs Dallow, who frowned severely at each of them, and by Mrs Collins, who fixed her own gaze with calm interest in the portrait of the late General Arthur Dallow on the wall opposite to her.

Mr Collins's compliments on every succeeding dish made it possible for the other diners to enjoy the dinner undisturbed. Later, when the gentlemen joined the ladies in the drawing-room, and Mrs Dallow saw that George and Bernard signalled dismay and merriment to Philippa, she said with some firmness:

"I suggest that we now have some music." She had found George, since the departure of the party to Bath, irrepressible, and herself could not account for his geniality. She felt this evening that, if he had infected even Bernard Phillips with his levity, the present occasion was in danger of collapse. "Miss Collins, would you be good enough to play for us?"

Marcia was unprepared for such a request. "I am afraid I do not play at all well, ma'am, and I have brought no music with me —"

"My daughter," pronounced Mr Collins, "wishes nothing less than to appear at all disobliging, ma'am, and is wholly sensible of the honour you pay her in asking her to perform on what I can perceive to be a noble instrument. She has no talent at all that can be compared with that of such young ladies as your daughters, who have had the advantage of superior tuition and of your own doubtless impeccable taste and guidance. She has had the best education that I have been able to provide for her, and although she is, as you observe, modest, that is not unfitting in a young girl and you will not mistake the quality, in your magnanimity, for stubborness. She is of a tractable disposition and will be happy to place her gifts, such as they are, at your disposal. Marcia, do as Mrs Dallow asks, if you please."

"Come," said Philippa kindly to Marcia, "there may be, among the music here, some piece that you know." She jumped up from the sofa and led Marcia to the pianoforte. "Oh, these are Mrs Ingle's books of songs; they should have been returned to her when Silvia left. Only she and Robert used them. You know Robert Pavey, do you not? While Silvia was with us, he came up once or twice and they sang together. He has not a bad voice."

"We are indeed," put in Mr Collins, "well acquainted with the Pavey family. They are as kind to us as you are, ma'am, in granting us the favour of their hospitality, and we are engaged very soon to dine there. Mr Robert, you will be aware, is a colleague of my son's. They work together in Mr Pavey's legal firm, and Mr Pavey is very much pleased with my son's ability and application. I am much indebted to Mr Pavey for taking my son as an articled pupil. It has been a part of my misfortune, that I could not provide for my only son. My means would not suffice for a university education – Not, naturally," he interrupted himself, "that I intend any complaint, and I should deplore it were you to misunderstand me. I am not speaking of my present position. The living is an excellent one, and I am most deeply thankful to Mr Dallow for bestowing it upon me. The Rectory is a most satisfactory dwelling in almost every way, and everything about the parish conduces to my happiness and renders me daily more grateful to my patron." He bowed to Mrs Dallow and, before she could speak, proceeded: "I should be lacking in humility and respect, where I not to profess myself content to pass the remainder of my life in the fulfilment of my duties here. My misfortune, to which I referred, arises from another direction. I have expectations in whose satisfaction there has been excessive delay. I have told you, I believe, that I am heir to a considerable estate in another part of the country. Only one elderly cousin stands between me and possessions that would relieve me of all anxiety. My son, in consequence, is deprived in his turn. He should, by right, be in a position similar to that of your own elder son, heir to a substantial property and learning the affairs of its surveillance, instead of being employed in a subordinate situation – Grateful as I am to Mr Pavey, and much as my son, also, appreciates Mr Pavey's generosity. William is of a humble and diligent disposition and will submit dutifully to the ordinances of such a career as is open to him."

William had lowered the greater part of his blushing face into his coffee-cup. When Mr Collins said: "You concur in what I say, do you not, William?" William muttered:

"Yes, sir."

"Miss Collins," called Mrs Dallow with a hint of urgency, "is there not perhaps a piece you could play from memory? We should be happy to hear any simple thing."

"Yes," cried Philippa, whose cheeks were pinker than William's, "please play anything."

"She will do so," affirmed Mr Collins.

Marcia, understanding the appeal if not its cause, sat at the pianoforte and played, obediently, a minuet she could remember from her early music lessons. Generously admired, she went on to another piece. She played well, unaffectedly, and if she commanded no brilliance of execution, none was in this instance required. George clapped his hands when she ended.

"George, you frightened Miss Collins," his mother reproved him. "A gentler method of approbation would have been more fitting."

"I am sorry, ma'am," said Marcia. She did not know what she might have betrayed, sensitive as she was to any movement from George's vicinity. The clapping of his hands had made her start violently.

"Do not apologise, my dear; it is for George to do that."

"Miss Collins, I apologise."

"No applogy is due to my daughter," declared Mr Collins. "Mr George may express his approval as he wishes, in his own house, and it is most flattering to my daughter that he condescends to do so. She is aware that she too has lacked opportunities of improvement that would have been hers, had my family not been prevented from enjoying its due. I do not intend to imply, I need not say, that I regret my elderly cousin's sustained good health. It would not behove me as a Christian to wish him other than a long life."

Bernard Phillips, who was enjoying this evening with a vivacity unusual in him, now said, for George's amusement and with no thought of tact: "If your cousin is a Christian too, sir, he may not think that it behoves him to exceed his allotted span."

Mr Collins replied with gravity: "He has done so. He was seventy-one years old last March."

"George, and Philippa," cried Mrs Dallow with an edge of anger to her voice, and with an intentional double meaning, "you are doing nothing to contribute to the success of our little party. Philippa, you must play for us now."

"But Mama, the Rondo in G has never yet contributed to the success of a party. Very well," she added, recognising the real sternness of her mother's face, "I will play it, but as fast as possible, to have done with it." Seating herself at the instrument she rattled through the rondo at a breakneck pace, missing many of the notes, urging on the music as she might have galloped her pony downhill as a child. Marcia watched in amazement. Mrs Dallow frowned. When the piece ended in a crashing approximation of the correct chord, George cried:

"Surely one should clap one's hands after that achievement. The piece can never have been performed in such a way before."

"Exactly what I was about to say myself," declared Mr Collins, who had been rehearsing his compliments rather than listening to the music. "Such taste and execution are rarely combined. Allow me to congratulate you, Miss Philippa, upon your musicianship, and you too, ma'am," turning to Mrs Dallow, "upon the evident care that had been lavished upon the nourishment of so conspicuous a talent."

There was a silence as of stupefaction. Mrs Dallow looked round for support; Bernard's face was crimson; George had compressed his features into a sort of funereal grimace; Philippa had thrust her handkerchief into her mouth and was shaking from head to foot. All at once, Mrs Dallow reached the end of her endurance. She broke helplessly into laughter, which she strove to conceal by placing her hands over her face. This placed an ultimate strain on the composure of Bernard, who was attacked with an apparent fit of coughing, and Philippa, who threw herself upon the sofa to the ruin of her hair-dressing. George retained presence of mind enough to seize the poker and prod needlessly at the coals.

"My dear madam," exclaimed Mr Collins rising, "what is the matter? Are you unwell?"

Mrs Dallow, ashamed, struggled with vigour against her

laughter and subdued it. She would not for anything have distressed Mrs Collins by such a display as this. "I am quite well, I thank you. I may have felt a sudden chill. Yes, George, please build up the fire. Philippa, go and pin up your hair. Bernard, please offer Mrs Collins more coffee, or some wine."

Composure was resumed. All those who had lapsed wished to make amends and the evening ended soberly as Mr Collins embarked on a speech of thanks that specified each detail of his entertainment.

During the unseemly outbreak of mirth, Mrs Collins had kept her eyes fixed serenely on a water-colour landscape beside the chimneypiece. Marcia, who had been still standing by the pianoforte after watching Philippa's galloping fingers, had had her back to the room and noticed nothing amiss except that Mrs Dallow had appeared briefly to be unwell, which in a lady of her regard for health would be sufficient to cause consternation in all present. Mr Collins had noticed nothing.

The one to suffer, and grievously, from the incident was William. The shock to him was so deep that for some time he could not identify his own feeling. That people should laugh at his father – and it had been clear to him that, simply, such an event had occurred – was more than unacceptable to him; it was incredible. Derision is belittling; there is no escaping that. But William did not believe it possible that his father, revered authority of his own life, could be belittled. In a painful daze, he stood by while his father uttered in the hallway of the manor yet another speech of thanks. As in a form of stupor he set out to accompany his family home, he strove in his stupor to suppress a rising agony that was as final as that of a bereavement.

When the door of the Hall was closed behind the guests

George remarked: "I enjoy Mr Collins. He is so ludicrous."

"You made that all too plain, George," remonstrated his mother. "But who am I to reproach you? We all behaved very badly."

"Do not trouble yourself, Mama. He is too obtuse to have noticed that we laughed at him. I am sorry, however, for Mr William and Miss Marcia. I should not care to have him for a father."

"Take care that you do not let them see that," Mrs Dallow warned him. "They are good young people, and would not admit disrespect for him from anyone."

"Well, I do not suppose we shall meet them often," said Philippa, "so it will not arise."

NINE

William Collins bore in solitude what was, in effect, the grief of disillusionment in his father. He could not confide in his mother or Marcia a sentiment potentially so subversive. He was sunk in sorrow and guilt, and too much cast down to ask himself why he need feel guilty. It could not strike him that, if he minded so much that the Dallows laughed at his father, it was because a part of him secretly agreed that they had reason to.

His mood, doleful as it had recently been, was not marked as altered by his family, nor in the office of Pavey and Son, the less so as the mood of Robert Pavey had become doleful in an extreme. His parents observed this but did not connect it with the departure of Miss Webster. They had always understood their son very well, but failed to understand how far this depended on his own openness. He had been used to tell them everything and they would have supposed that, falling in love, he would have been eager to share his feelings with them. With a first love, however, and particularly in one of Robert Pavey's normally easy nature, there can arise a desire for privacy of feeling; this is not the same thing as secretiveness, but is a necessity for the growth of inward experience. After the happy hours spent over the song books, Robert was left to a melancholy that was new to him, and more poetic than desperate, although to an observer the effects were not distinguishable.

"I do not know what can be the matter," said Mrs Pavey. "Can he be ill?"

"I am still afraid he may not be satisfied by his work," Mr Pavey reiterated. When he asked Robert, Robert insisted that he was as glad as ever to be the 'and Son' of the brass plate.

"Then I fear your mother is right, and you are not quite well. I do not like to see you so quiet. Come, Robert, try to look forward. There is the public ball next week, for instance. And I am sure some fresh air would help revive you. Tomorrow, take a free day, and go hunting with George Dallow. Thomas says they are drawing the manor woods, and your horse must need the exercise also. You have been out so little lately."

The excursion did Robert no good. The day was dark, the ground muddy, the sport poor, but, worst of all, George himself inflicted on Robert a crushing blow, as, dusk approaching, they waited beside the wood for a strayed couple of hounds. Robert, who had had no opportunity all day to raise the topic dearest to him, now remarked that he hoped all the friends in Bath were happy, and inquired in an incidental fashion whether Miss Webster might visit Teverton again soon?

"I expect so," said George in a casual tone, adding: "I am to marry her, you know." At once he shouted: "There they go!" as the pair of hounds leapt over the wall some way below, and, cracking his whip, he turned his horse in pursuit and cantered off down the wood side. Robert did not follow, but turned his own horse homeward through the rain.

The melancholy that Robert had suffered was as nothing to the dejection that overtook him after George's announcement. He had had no thought himself of marriage

with Miss Webster and would have supposed her
unattainable in any case; but now, that she was lost to him
before he had more than distantly adored her made her loss
the more severe. The prospect of next week's public ball did
less than ever to cheer him, and when the evening arrived,
and the guests from Teverton Rectory ascended the stairs
to the drawing-room above the offices of Pavey and Son,
Robert could not summon a smile as he bowed to the
ladies.

Mr Collins smiled upon everything and did not cease to
dilate upon his awareness of his hosts' condescension and
the excellence of his dinner. In the drawing-room again, he
told his son:

"William, you are too slow with your thanks and
compliments to your benefactors. These are not office
hours, you realise, and Mr and Mrs Pavey may expect a
little more freedom of manner, within the bounds of
decorum, than is normal. However, they will be tolerant,
and allow for youth and shyness. Towards Mr Robert, with
whom you are on more informal terms, if he will permit me
to say so, I am sure you will wish to show your
appreciation, by giving him your permission, humbly and
suitably, to engage your sister to dance."

"Yes, sir," replied William.

Mr Collins looked towards his son to elaborate on his
speech, but Robert, recognising that Fitz was unable to,
recollected himself and requested Miss Collins for the
honour of the opening dance. He could do no other. It was
all one to him, with whom he danced, or whether he danced
at all; as anyone, watching his demeanour in the Assembly
Room, could have divined.

The room was crowded. Sir Edgar Bewley had brought a
large party and several strangers were present. In all the
laughter and chatter, Robert's silence was conspicuous.

Marcia tried to initiate conversation with him, without success. Presently she said:

"If you do not wish to talk, Mr Robert, I shall be silent."

"Please do not. – Be silent, that is. I am sorry. I am afraid I am not in talkative mood this evening."

"I fancied that Miss Browne thought it strange, when you did not reply to her greeting."

"Did Elizabeth speak to me? I did not notice it."

Marcia ventured after a moment: "I am afraid you are more than untalkative, Mr Robert. You are in low spirits."

"Yes, I cannot make myself cheerful just now. But I am sorry you find me poor company. It is good of you to bear with me."

Marcia disclaimed. She tried to encourage him to persist in converation by remarking: "It is unusual not to see the Miss Dallows at a ball, is it not. Only Miss Philippa is here. I believe she came with Mr Joseph Browne, and not with Mr George Dallow; him, I do not see."

"Please do not speak to me of George Dallow," implored Robert with a heavy sigh. "I am glad he is not come tonight. Of all people I desire least to meet him." A quickness of inquiry in Miss Collins's eyes made him add: "He told me, a day or so ago, that he is engaged to marry his cousin Miss Webster." Having uttered this, Robert tightened his lips, as if that concluded the subject. Marcia was left to deduce for herself the significance to him of the statement.

Whatever its significance to her, she set it aside. It did not call for great power of deduction, to associate Miss Webster's engagement with Mr Robert's low spirits, and Marcia could sympathise with him. She endeavoured to do so by saying:

"I am sorry you are unhappy."

"It is not upon their account, I assure you," returned

Robert with too much emphasis to carry conviction. "I
have only a slight acquaintance with Miss Webster, and no
claim upon her. As for George, I wish him all happiness.
Only I wonder that, friends as we are, he did not tell me
sooner of the matter."

"Can it be that they have formed a secret engagement?"

"I do not see why they should do that."

"Nor I. But it is strange, that there has been no
announcement."

"It will come. Until it does, I shall not advertise the
news."

"Then I had better not speak of it to anyone, either,"
Marcia suggested. "There must be good cause, for such an
important and happy occasion not to be made public by the
Dallows."

"The cause does not concern me," returned Robert, with
the air of one weary of discussion. Marcia therefore let the
topic rest and they progressed down the set in a resumed
silence. Robert did, nevertheless, feel a little more at ease
after confessing the source of his wretchedness. He began to
think Fitz's sister a tactful and understanding girl. He
could bear to dance with her, although he could not match
the gaiety of any of the other young ladies with whom he
would as a rule have danced. Marcia was his only partner
of the evening. He cared to ask no one else and she had
neither the unkindness nor the courage to refuse him. Once
or twice Robert left the ballroom to pace the corridor
outside and listen to the rain beating upon the shutters;
meanwhile, Marcia danced with William; but when Robert
returned, resigning himself again to the duty of sociability,
he approached Marcia as if she were a refuge from it.

As the Rectory carriage travelled homeward, Mr Collins
was upon the whole well pleased with his evening. Lady
Bewley had remembered meeting him before; the Paveys

had been most gracious; his wife and children must write notes of thanks for their dinner, tomorrow morning, and William must take them with him into Fraxted. "But you, William," Mr Collins said, thus reminded, "I am not satisfied with. You are now twenty years old. When do you intend to grow out of your loutishness? While we were at dinner, I do not believe you uttered one word. Those are not the manners expected in such company and I am disappointed again in you."

William had suffered grievously throughout the same dinner, trying not to observe his father through the eyes of the Paveys, nor to listen with their ears to his father's fulsomeness. The terrible doubts instilled by the laughter of the Dallows had but been confirmed. William was tormented by the looming spectre of his father's absurdity, but his honesty could not banish it. He remained silent.

"Do you not hear me, William? Are you deaf, as well as tongue-tied? I gave you every opportunity of offering a graceful and complimentary speech, when I hinted that you beg Mr Robert to ask Marcia to dance. I can do no more than I do, to assist you. Why did you not speak?"

"But, Father," said William in the first impulse of rebellion in his life, "it was not for me to advise Mr Robert in his choice of partner."

"Nor is it for you, sir," cried Mr Collins astonished, "to advise *me* on what is or is not the acceptable social gesture. You are stubborn, William. Stubborn you may be, but insolence, in addition, I will not tolerate. I see I shall have to attend still to your manners." He did not wish, however, to spoil his own recollections of the evening in dwelling upon William's shortcomings. He turned to his daughter. "Marcia, you acquitted yourself well. I thank you, my dear girl. You have made, if I may employ a well-worn phrase, a conquest this evening, of Mr Robert."

"I do not think so, Papa."

"Do not let me find you like your brother, Marcia, in disagreeing with me in that impudent fashion. It was noticed that Mr Robert danced with you exclusively Did he not, my love?" he appealed to Mrs Collins.

"He was most attentive," was all that Mrs Collins would say, in a conciliatory tone. She did not wish to discuss Robert Pavey in front of Marcia and was herself awaiting leisure for reflection before deciding whether or not to be pleased with his attentiveness; it had been too sudden and complete to comply with either the conventions of a public ball, or the manners of a young gentleman initiating a courtship. It was beyond doubt, nonetheless, that Mr Robert had been attentive, and when she was with her husband in private, Mrs Collins began by her own methods to ensure that Mr Robert's possible suit should not be discouraged by Mr Collins's encouraging it. When he referred to Marcia's 'conquest', Mrs Collins said:

"Yes, everyone noticed that Mr Robert singled out Marcia. I am sure she was sensible of the honour. The Paveys are very respectable people, and although Mr Robert was said to be wild at Oxford, he is grown more steady in these last years. It would be a suitable connection, as things are. Of course, were we living in Hertfordshire, as by now you hoped we should be, our own position would be such, that we could look higher for her. But she is eighteen now, and these matters cannot wait for ever."

Thus she turned Mr Collins's mind into its regular channel of discontents and let him remind her that it appeared they were to wait for ever, such was his misfortune, through no fault of his own. On the next day, she spoke to Marcia.

"I do not think he was strongly attracted to me," said Marcia with candour. "He was in no mood for dancing with any of the pretty girls."

"My dear, do not be cynical, and do not underrate yourself. Where you not pleased, that he paid you such attention? Do you like him?"

"Yes, I do, Mama, and I was pleased that he told me – That is, I was glad to ..." Marcia checked herself, unable to explain that she had been of some small service to Mr Robert in sympathising with his trouble; since she could not explain the trouble to her mother, she had better say nothing. Mrs Collins did not press the question. From a consciousness in Marcia's hesitation, her mother permitted herself the hope that, whatever Marcia was keeping from her, it accorded with her own wishes for her daughter's future.

TEN

The letters Mrs Dallow received from her daughters in Bath spoke of clothes, concerts and balls; Walter, adding brief postscripts, said nothing of his cough. The visit was expected to extend until Christmas, by which time Mr Dallow hoped to return home also. When Mrs Dallow was told that Mrs Forbes's house stood higher than the town centre, and that country walks were included in her family's activities, she was resigned to the separation.

For others, this autumn and winter offered only dullness. Dark days and wet weather kept Robert despondent, and William had damp walks to and from the dreary office. For hours, Robert stared out of the window of that office at an empty street. On a day without rain, he saw nothing more eventful than the arrival of the Rectory chaise at Thompson's the drapers; Mrs Collins and her daughter alighted and passed within. Soon, Miss Collins emerged alone and walked quickly down the street; she entered the ironmonger's. Sighing, Robert picked up his pen; but another character stepped upon the stage of the drama: George Dallow, on his roan mare, trotted into sight. The drama heightened: At the same moment Miss Collins came out again from the ironmonger's and George, seeing her, dismounted and spoke to her. The mare blocked Robert's view, but he could see two heads nodding towards each other in what seemed earnest colloquy. Curiosity stirred in Robert.

What he could not hear was this: George began:

"Miss Collins – Good-day to you – May I speak with you? I believe your brother is still seeing Robert daily. Has he any idea of what is wrong with the man?"

"With Mr Robert?" asked Marcia, much surprised.

"I'd be obliged if you could find out. Robert has not been near me for weeks – Indeed, I am sure he is avoiding me in the town. I am not going to risk a rebuff by asking Robert direct. We were pretty good friends all our lives, you know, until one day when we were hunting, when he rode off home without a word, leaving me to collect up the hounds as best I might. Has he taken some fit? Ask your brother, will you?"

"Indeed, Mr Dallow," cried Marcia, "I had much rather not undertake any such commission. You must excuse me."

"Well, I expect if Robert were annoyed with me, he would not explain it to your brother in any case. I suppose I must confront Robert –"

Marcia, uncertain of the ways of gentlemen in George Dallow's world when a lady was at issue, envisaged duelling pistols. "I do not think that would be wise," she said in anxiety.

"Oh; so you know that there is trouble between us, do you? And you know the reason for it?" George challenged her.

"No – I know nothing. That is – I had much rather you did not speak of it to me," protested Marcia in confusion.

"You have been kind to me before now," said George. "I should have thought I might depend on you to help me."

"You must forgive me – I should dearly like to help, if I could – But it would not help matters, were I to betray a confidence –"

"Oh. So that is what passes for discretion, in the daughter of a clergyman," said George out of temper. "Well, I will not trouble you again. And Robert may avoid me, for all I care. I can do very well without him. Good-day." He mounted his horse and turned back in the direction from which he had come, sparks springing from the cobbles under the whirling hooves.

George's rebuke threw Marcia into an agitation evident even from the distance of Robert's window. Robert, seeing her walk slowly up the street with reddened cheeks, dashing away tears with her muff, jumped up from his desk and hurried through the vestibule. Crossing the street to Marcia's side he asked without greeting:

"What has George been saying, to distress you?"

The sudden unceremonious appearance of Mr Robert, hatless, added to Marcia's dismay. She could say only: "Nothing – It was nothing." Then, lest he too should accuse her of 'discretion' in some derogatory sense, she forced herself to add: "He regrets that you are not friendly to him now. But, naturally, that is no concern of mine –"

"I see no reason for you to be caught up in any quarrel between us," said Robert touching her hand. "I am sorry for it and do not know why George should mention it to you. Nor do I see why he should pretend he does not know why it is painful to me to meet him nowadays. He is too much used to having his own way, and that renders him inconsiderate. Think nothing of him." With that advice, he left her and hurried back to the office.

The latter of these encounters had been witnessed by Mrs Collins, as she came out of the draper's and stood in the doorway while the assistant carried her purchases to the chaise. She saw Marcia's distress, and Robert's touch of her hand, and wondered what had passed between the two of them. She did not inquire and self-command enabled

Marcia to spare her mother from a daughter's tearfulness in the middle of the town. Approaching, she told her mother that the lamp was not yet mended.

"Then we shall go straight on to the butcher's," said Mrs Collins, as if she had noticed nothing amiss, for which Marcia was thankful. She could not accept Robert's advice and 'think nothing of' George Dallow; George's burst of anger kept her trembling inwardly for the rest of that day.

George himself had felt immediate remorse for his treatment of Miss Collins, but dispersed it in the resentment he felt towards Robert. With Robert especially George had been used to leading, and to having his own way; any initiative in desertion, as in anything, should have come from George. Pride, as well as indolence, prevented George's making any further attempt to mend the breach between them. He missed Robert, all the same. In the absence of Walter and two of his sisters, he lacked an audience.

One evening as he drove homeward in his curricle, its lamp picked out a figure plodding along the roadside in the mud. George recognised young Collins and drew up to offer him a ride, not sorry to find some company. Nor was William sorry to be relieved of his walk in the rain, which had become inevitable now that Mr Robert did not visit Teverton in the evenings. He thanked Mr George, relieved too that Mr George would not expect the thanks to be expressed after the manner of the senior Mr Collins.

"I have been to look at a gun dog over by Blackhill," George told him. "Well trained, they had told me – but the brute was a hundred years old and has lost half its teeth." Living as usual in the moment, George did not think to inquire after Robert, nor remember why the Collins family hovered again on the brink of his conscience. As he went on with the tale of the unworthy gun dog, William laughed without constraint, rendered at ease by George's own ease and the headlong pace of the curricle through the dark rain. "I will tell you what I was about to do," said George at the Rectory gate. "I wanted to drench the black gelding, but I am late, and the grooms will have gone to their dinner. Would you come and help me? Then you can see my foal, and report to your sister how it is thriving."

William was much interested to see the stables of the manor. Since the dinner-party there, whereat his father had announced him to be heir of an estate comparable to George Dallow's, William had for the first time begun to wonder about, though not to believe in, the fabled property in Hertfordshire. At the moment, in addition, he was ready to seize at any pretext for delaying his return home, where he was so constantly troubled by his own treacherous misery. He asked so many questions of George about the running of stables and farms, that George found his audience and was cheered by it. "You must see the kennels, and the mill," he offered. "But you must come in daylight. This evening it is too late."

Too late William was for the family dinner, which earned him a lengthy reproof from his father. William would have been glad to tell them at home about his adventure, and the affability of Mr George, and the quantity of oats consumed in the Tevertons tables; for once, William had something to say; but Mr Collins was interested in no excuses, nor, William could not but feel, in William's activities. A spark of resentment was kindled: Very well then, William said to himself, I will tell you nothing. He was not perhaps as guilty as he should have been, in having allowed the resentment, for that spark had lit for the first time a possible way of escape: it might be possible to find a way of life outside his father's domination? In twenty years the possibility had not presented itself and William was afraid to pursue it.

He apologised to his mother for his lateness and told Marcia: "Mr George showed me his bay mare's foal, and asked me to tell you that it grows strong."

Marcia was by now well on her guard against sudden mention of George Dallow. She longed to ask: "How was it that you saw the foal, and Mr George?" and William longed to tell her; but instead, Marcia said: "I am glad to hear that," in so cool a tone that William extended to her the truculence he had felt towards his father, and said no more.

George Dallow, reminded of young Collins by seeing him in church on the next Sunday, was reminded of his offer and carried off William at once to the mill. At this time of year, if William were to do anything in daylight it must perforce be upon a Sunday. Again, William was ready with questions over all he saw. Some of them, George was unable to answer. How, for instance, did he know the amount of seed corn to be issued for sowing? "Oh," replied George, "I leave all that to the bailiff. I cannot trouble myself with such details." He told William that, according the steward, fifty sacks of barley had been laid in the granary. William observed: "I do not see fifty sacks, I think."

"Do not be so scrupulous, Collins. Fifty or forty, what matter. But now you point it out, he said he had entered fifty in the ledger, yet I see ... Wait ... They are not arranged tidily; there should be five rows of ten, is that correct? Let us count them ..." The two young men hauled the sacks to and fro, covering William's Sunday coat with a fine embellishment of dust. The final reckoning was either forty-seven or forty-eight sacks, they could not exactly decide. "In either case, I am d – d if I will be cheated by these fellows. I have been too easy with them altogether," George declared. It did not please him that he should be shown up before young Collins as an inefficient master. He took the blame of it, however, upon himself and was not unappreciative of William's interest. "Come, Fitz," he said at last, dropping into the use of the name he had been used to hear Robert employ, "you cannot go home so tousled. You must come indoors and have your coat brushed, and take a glass of wine, or you will develop a cough like my brother's, in all the chaff you have breathed."

William gave his coat to be brushed, but omitted to attend in the same way to his hair; so that, when he had run down the lane to arrive late home, the collar of his coat was again in a condition that could not escape his mother's notice. Apologising for it, William had to explain the circumstances, and Mr Collins listening exclaimed:

"Sacks of corn! Is that a fit occupation for the Sabbath day, sir?"

"I suppose it is not. But I have no other opportunity."

"William, I will not have this answering-back. I perceive a spirit of insolence in you that I will not tolerate. You would do well to be silent when reproved deservedly."

"But Mr George asked me to help him, sir. I could not refuse."

"Be silent, sir."

William obeyed an injunction which his father had for twenty years exhorted him to disobey. Mrs Collins said:

"It was wrong of Mr George to lead William astray, but we know that Mr George's manners are not yours, my love."

"Precisely so. My family owes it to me to set an example in the parish."

"Yes, indeed. William will refuse to help Mr George henceforward."

William looked askance at his mother. It was not her habit to refuse help to anyone, nor to enjoin her children to do so. He could not guess, in his own simplicity, that she had hoped to provoke her husband into saying what he promptly said:

"Such a refusal would set no example. Scripture tells us that an ox may be lifted from a pit upon the Sabbath, and Mr George may, I give it upon the authority of my cloth, be included in such a category. In addition, I expect my son to demonstrate his willingness to be of any service, at any time, to the family of my patron, little as my own patient assiduities have achieved in that direction." Upon reflection, Mr Collins was not altogether pleased that William should be upon such intimate terms with Mr George Dallow and the Hall, when he himself had not yet insinuated himself there. Mrs Collins, however, noticing that William was much improved in animation and energy under Mr George's attentions, wished the friendship to develop.

It was doing George Dallow no harm, to have someone stimulate his interest in estate affairs. One evening he collected William in the town and took him to call on Bernard Phillips, who had been talking of buying a tract of woodland from the Teverton borders. "You must look solemn, Fitz," George adjured him, "and I shall say that I have brought my legal advisor. Mind, I have no authority to sell land in my father's absence, but I want to show Bernard that I can be as grave as he, when I am so inclined." A couple of bottles of wine among the young men somewhat marred the gravity of the discussion, but an agreeable evening was passed, and William, delivered back at the Rectory after the doors had been locked, took his father's reproof almost as a matter of course.

Mrs Collins said to Marcia: "You father does not like it, that William has been taken up by George Dallow; but, for myself, I see it as no bad thing. What do you think of it?"

"I see no harm in Mr George, and William seems happy to be with him," Marcia replied in so neutral a tone that Mrs Collins was reassured that Marcia, at any rate, was free now of Mr George's toils.

The two fathers, Mr Collins and Mr Pavey, were now on opposite sides of the same question: Mr Pavey, who used to wish that his son would see less of George Dallow, now wished, observing Robert so dejected, that he would see more of him again; while Mr Collins, observing William so cheerful, wished that he would see less.

ELEVEN

Mrs Forbes had been widowed very young and at a time wherein her family was suffering financial misfortune. To avoid being a burden on them, she had taken the post of companion to Miss Mallory. It had been intended that Mrs Forbes should return to her family – a highly respectable one – as soon as her father's affairs were mended; or, it had been supposed by many, she would remarry. In the event, such an affection grew between her and Miss Mallory, and between Mrs Forbes and the orphaned great-niece Silvia, that the household became a contented permanency. After the death of Miss Mallory, Mrs Forbes had no thought of giving up Silvia. From Miss Mallory's legacy to her she purchased a smaller house in Bath and prepared to devote herself to Silvia until Silvia married.

Over this, Mrs Forbes was vigilant. Silvia's parents, and her great-aunt, had elevated her to the status of heiress and, in such a place as Bath, eligible but acquisitive young men were numerous. Mrs Forbes set Silvia's happiness above every other consideration, but was doubtful that she could have said the same for Silvia's absentee legal guardian in Essex, nor for Silvia's attentive brother Henry, whom Mrs Forbes had invited to look upon her house in Bath as his home. Henry often appeared there, usually unannounced and accompanied by a brother officer or two, of whom he confided to Mrs Forbes: "What say you to Lionel" (or Leonard, or Ludovic) "as a husband for Silvia? He is a capital fellow and a great friend of mine."

When three of the cousins visited from Essex, all could not be accommodated in Mrs Forbes's house, fortunate as it was that Henry's regiment should be quartered nearby at the time. Walter went into lodgings with Henry and his friend Thomas Godfrey, which added much to Walter's enjoyment of his visit. Tales of army life kept him up for half of each night.

In Mrs Forbes's house, equal harmony reigned. Mrs Forbes had been a little apprehensive of the arrival of these cousins who had, as she well knew, terrified Silvia in childhood; but she was relieved to find Corinna and Jane, though lively, pleasant in their manners, and Silvia quite at ease with them. Corinna and Jane, for their part, had been relieved to find Mrs Forbes so personable and liberal; they had expected some mittened old governess, or fat and fussy matron. No restraint was laid upon their pleasures; they chose what they wanted in the shops, and walked where they wished in the countryside, although the autumn weather was as damp here as in Essex, and few other visitors to Bath ventured afield. Corinna had promised her mother that she and her sister would take regular exercise, however, and the promise they kept. They had the advantage of the escort of Admiral Lawrence, an old friend of Mrs Forbes's late husband, who was familiar with the driest and prettiest paths and was willing to accompany the young ladies. When they went to evening balls, they made a large and cheerful party; the time passed very pleasantly for all.

Henry Webster noticed that his young sister showed herself more animated, and hence more beautiful, among this company than he had ever known her. He was not surprised that his friend Thomas Godfrey felt mightily attracted towards her.

This Thomas Godfrey had been a close friend of Henry for quite three weeks before Henry decided on him as a suitable husband for Silvia. He was a young man of outstandingly handsome appearance, small fortune, good family and venturesome disposition. His courage in action had been remarkable and he longed for the regiment to be active in battle again. He liked nothing better than to describe campaigns he had taken part in and battles he hoped to win hereafter. His political views were simple: Let the army have its way with his country's enemies and peace would be established for ever.

"Do you not think," Henry asked Mrs Forbes, "that Godfrey is the most splendid fellow?"

"I find him enthusiastic and charming, yes."

"And do you not think him enthusiastic about Silvia?"

"I had not thought so. Indeed, at first, I fancied him attracted to Corinna."

"Oh, no, that is not true. Corinna may appeal more immediately to a stranger – But all her charm lies on the surface. Godfrey is coming to value the quieter beauty of Silvia. You will see what comes of it."

"Do not be over-hopeful, Henry, that anything will."

Henry was, nevertheless, hopeful and did all in his power to further his friend's cause. Silvia appeared to accept Thomas Godfrey's attentions readily, praised him highly when Henry required her to and bloomed gracefully in Godfrey's company. Henry began to speak of their marriage, to his cousins, as virtually a settled thing. When, after an evening at the theatre, Thomas Godfrey confided to Henry that he had offered himself to Miss Webster during the intermission and had been gently rejected, Henry was hurt on his own account as well as on his friend's.

"But why should she refuse you?" he demanded.

"She told me, she does not wish to marry yet."

"Is that all? Then there is still hope. You must persevere!"

It might now be explained, for the illumination of the reader if not of the protagonists in this story, that no engagement existed yet between Silvia Webster and George Dallow. When George told Robert Pavey at the wood side: "I am to marry her, you know," he had interrupted himself on sighting the elusive hounds; the remainder of his sentence would have been: "... or so my father intends."

Mr and Mrs Dallow both thought a connection between their eldest son and Silvia advisable and, on that visit of Silvia's, had told George so. They had always felt it would be convenient to keep Silvia's fortune within the family, but they were not mercenary; they had waited to see whether Silvia would develop suitably, before they offered the suggestion to George. Finding Silvia all they could desire, they had hinted very strongly to George that he make his proposal forthwith.

George too found his cousin altogether charming, lovely and accomplished. The only hindrance was that he was not inclined towards matrimony; or, not yet. Hence his low spirits and unsociable behaviour while Silvia was at Teverton, and a guilty relief when she had left, since he felt he had failed in a duty, without fully admitting it as such.

Silvia was, then, free to accept Thomas Godfrey. Henry would not see why she would not. "I begin to suspect you of obstinacy," he told his sister. "What can you find in Thomas that does not please you?"

"He is a very pleasing man. I admire him. He has been so kind to me."

"Then what can you have against him? I do not understand you. Thousands of girls would be delighted by a proposal from him."

"I am sure they would. I am grateful for his good opinion of me, but I feel I do not deserve it. Nor do I wish to marry."

"That, as a reason, is purely negative. You must overcome such wishes for Thomas's sake. It is unkind of you to disappoint him."

"Please do not think me obstinate or unkind," pleaded Silvia, tears filling her eyes. It was a fine morning and she was walking with her brother in the Crescent while at a little distance Thomas Godfrey, well aware that Henry was interceding for him, walked with Jane and Walter. They were all awaiting Corinna, who had to visit the milliner's. At a greater distance, Mrs Forbes and Admiral Lawrence strolled together. Henry indicated them to Silvia:

"If you will not consider Thomas, then at least have regard for your very dear friend Mrs Forbes. Should you not act out of gratitude for all she had done for you? Already she has sacrificed years of her life, and of possible happiness."

"What do you mean?" asked Silvia, uneasy.

"Surely you have realised that she and Admiral Lawrence want to marry."

"No – I have never thought of such a thing!"

"Think of it now. She has devoted herself to you, and will continue to do so, until you are off her hands. And now you have the chance to set her free. Trust me: Within a month of your marrying, you will hear that she and the Admiral are to make a wedding of it also."

Silvia's alarm and dismay at this idea overcame her. "I believe you are right, Henry. Why did I not think of it? How selfish I have been! And she – so unselfish! I have taken everything from her, and given nothing. I accepted her devotion, as you say, and I have never been allowed to

suspect more than a friendly attachment between her and
Admiral Lawrence. But, now that you point it out ..." She
walked on, flushed and trembling. Henry drew her hand
through his arm.

"Do not be troubled. I know Mrs Forbes loves you dearly
and has given you no more than she wished, or you
deserved. But other people, you know, could be as willing to
devote themselves to you, would you but allow it. Now, we
shall speak of this no longer. Let those tears stop; Mrs
Forbes would be angry with me if I made you unhappy.
But, if you consider what I have told you, then you might
mention Admiral Lawrence to her, in such a way as to gain
for yourself some measure of her feelings for him. You must
judge for yourself whether I am right."

He felt he could rely on Silvia's affection for Mrs Forbes,
to sway that judgement in the required direction.

TWELVE

It was about two weeks after that day that a letter to Mrs
Dallow from Silvia stated that she would like to ask Mr
Dallow's consent, as soon as he returned home, to her
marriage with Captain Thomas Godfrey. An
accompanying letter from Mrs Forbes proposed that, when
the young Dallows returned to Teverton, Silvia and
Captain Godfrey might be invited with them so that
Captain Godfrey could be introduced there. Letters from
Corinna and Jane spoke, more informally than either of the
others, of the Captain's good looks and valour.

Mrs Dallow's immediate response to the news was: "Oh,
George, Silvia is to marry some young man we have never
heard of! I am so sorry that you did not speak, while she
was here."

George's immediate reflection was rather of relief that he
had not. He wished his cousin Silvia every happiness and
visualised her now as even more beautiful than before –
indeed, far above him in elegance and style of life.
Meditating more freely upon marriage, as he rode round
the estate, he admitted that he could not have made Silvia
happy. If he were to have a wife – and surely, in good time,
he would – beauty and accomplishments were all very well,
but, for a lifetime's companion, he would rather choose
someone of practical good sense who shared his own

interests; someone for instance like Fitz's sister, Miss What-was-her-name. But, time enough for such matters. George was too busy for them, in his increasing concern with matters of the estate. It had begun to seem that these went amiss during his father's absences. Instead of roaming with his gun, George now was in the habit of riding to market to discover what price his pigs fetched, or even sending for the ledgers and having Fitz check them over for him. The two of them made many a late night of it over ledgers and wine, in the Teverton library; it was no concern of George's, nor did William mention, that whereas George might sleep off this labour the next morning until what hour he pleased, William must be at the office of Pavey and Son by his usual hour; which, too often nowadays, he was not.

There could be no official announcement of Silvia's engagement until Mr Dallow's consent was obtained, but nor was there any reason for concealment, and Mrs Dallow spoke of it to her friends as decided. Few among the neighbourhood knew Miss Webster at all well, and no one knew of her supposed betrothal to George Dallow, so the tidings did not travel as fast as if it had been a secret. The two who imagined themselves to be in possession of the secret of George's betrothal, Robert Pavey and Marcia Collins, heard of its refutation at the same moment. They were both at the Rectory, where the Collinses had invited the Paveys and the Ingles to dinner.

It was Mrs Ingle who divulged the information, but the dinner was well advanced before she was able to do so, so prolix were Mr Collins's apologies for the deficiencies of his hospitality while nevertheless contriving to praise its every item, and so profuse his apologies for the absence of his son, whose company, he strove to make plain, had been begged for by Mr George Dallow, who had flattered his son by making a great friend of him and seeking his assistance in many weighty affairs concerning the Teverton estates. "I feel it as much my son's duty," explained Mr Collins, "to wait upon Mr George Dallow, as to attend my own modest family party, and I earnestly hoped that none of my guests tonight will be affronted by his absence." No one was; nor was Mr Collins as certain of his son's whereabouts as he claimed. It was normally assumed now, at the Rectory, that when William failed to appear, he must be with George Dallow. William had been strictly commanded to appear at the family table this evening, and his failure to do so, his mother feared might be due to some accident; she did not believe that William would dare defy his father to this extent. In proportion as William was cheerful with George Dallow, he became more positively sullen towards his father, and Mrs Collins beheld this too with disquiet. She dreaded any conflict between the two, more especially as she knew that William was unlikely to be the victor.

During these musings of Mrs Collins, Mrs Ingle had at last gained the attention of the gathering and was announcing that the lace on her gown was of poorer quality than she liked, having come only from Thompson's, but the original lace her laundry-maid had ruined, and indeed she had turned off the maid, but not before securing the promise of another, a girl from Teverton, no longer needed there, and recommended by Mrs Dallow, whom Mrs Ingle had met at the Downings', the day before, and who had told her of Miss Webster's engagement to a soldier in Bath, which had pleased Mrs Ingle, who remembered how prettily Miss Webster had sung with Robert, which had reminded her of Robert's singing as a little boy at a party at her house, when her nephew was staying –

"Miss Webster is engaged?" cried Mrs Pavey. But Mrs Ingle had regressed already beyond her nephew to his father's fondness for billiards and the rest of the company could only exchange looks of surprise. Marcia, involuntarily, turned to look at Robert, and he at her; there was an evident understanding in their glances that Mrs Collins observed, though she could not have accounted for it, and it gratified her.

In the drawing-room, a card-table was made up, but the speeches of Mr Collins delayed the game for so long that Robert and Marcia were able to draw apart into a window and speak privately.

"Did you know anything of Miss Webster's marrying this soldier?" asked Robert at once.

"No, indeed – I am astonished!" cried Marcia. "I hope poor Mr George is not too sadly disappointed."

"Oh, who cares for George? He should have gone with her to Bath. If he has lost her, it is by his own fault."

If Marcia did care for George's disappointment, she was sympathetic enough with Robert not to say so. Robert had been disappointed twice over, which must be a double distress to him. "But I cannot suppose Miss Webster inconstant –"

"No, no. She would never be unfaithful. Her sentiments are too noble. Depend upon it, George will have released her from their engagement, knowing himself unworthy of her. And I suppose," added Robert in a morose tone, "this man in Bath is everything she could desire."

In supposing this, Robert considered his own sentiments not ignoble. He was condemning himself to final exclusion from Miss Webster's life. An imaginary suitor, worthy of her, was a greater impediment to any aspirations of Robert's than old George Dallow could ever be. Finality had reality; Robert was forced to admit that his dreams of Miss Webster had been but dreams. Sighing, he forced himself further to suppose that when Miss Webster married this excellent husband, she would not come again to Teverton and he would see her no more.

"I have been nothing but foolish," he said upon his sigh.

"Oh, do not say that. I understand very well how you must feel, and it is only that loving with no hope of return necessarily makes one ..." Marcia paused, searching for the word, and Robert took up:

"You understand? Yes, I believe you do."

"Oh, I imagine I understand," Marcia corrected herself with a blush. "I do not mean to intrude on your ... your hidden feeling –"

"*I* understand," said Robert almost smiling, "that you are discreet as well as sympathetic, and I am thankful to have at least one friend to whom I may speak of those hidden feelings."

It was true, he had come to depend on Miss Collins's sympathy; he had had no one else to talk to. George had apparently taken up young Fitz in Robert's place and Fitz himself seemed half asleep in the office for most of the day.

William did not return, that evening, until after midnight. Mr Collins waited up for him, but Mrs Collins preferred to retire. The next morning she sent the servant twice to wake William, before going herself to rouse him.

"I wonder we have had no report from Mr Pavey, William, of your arriving there so often late in the mornings," she said. "I hope you are making up the work to his satisfaction."

"I do not greatly care. I do not care for the work either."

After a moment Mrs Collins said: "Take care, please, William, that you do not cause any trouble between the Paveys and our family, for Marcia's sake."

William did not know, or ask, what she implied. He did not know what his sister had to do with Robert Pavey.

It now wanted but a few weeks to Christmas. Mr Dallow was soon expected at Teverton and according to rumour the party from Bath, to include Miss Webster and her dashing captain, would be not far behind him. Meanwhile, the neighbourhood was to be enlivened by nothing more than a visit to the Paveys by Mrs Pavey's brother and his wife, from Nottingham. During this, the Paveys were to give a dinner-party, but the Collinses were not invited. They, and some others, were asked to drink tea in the evening.

Mr Collins was ready to be slighted, particularly since he had but recently had the Paveys at his own table. "This is offensive. Are we to be treated like the Miss Fishers or old Mr King, or others of no account in the town? In all humility, I must take a stand here, and plead a prior engagement. The Paveys need not presume that we are to run to and fro at their pleasure."

Alarmed by his recklessness of the Paveys' favour, Mrs Collins chose to give her husband a hint of her own reasons for wishing to preserve friendly relations with them. Mr Collins was incredulous.

"You fancy there is an attachment between Marcia and Robert Pavey? But you were the first to deny that she had made a conquest of him, at the public ball. Nor has he pursued his suit in any way. Nor did you think it desirable that he should."

Poor Mrs Collins was caught in her own toils, but said with no admission of it: "I speak of it only as a possibility, my love. And you know, there is William to be thought of. For his sake too, we should not show any ingratitude to the Paveys."

Effectively distracted, Mr Collins expostulated: "William! Why should I pay any regard to his interests, when he pays none to them himself? I receive nothing from him but insolence, negligence and base ingratitude – And speaking of that, I do not know how you dare mention ingratitude in connection with myself. Upon my word as a Christian, I have done all I could, upon every occasion, and in every association, throughout my life, to show more than adequate appreciation of every benefit conferred upon me. That is a rule of conduct that I have kept with the utmost scrupulousness and it disappoints me, it stabs me in the heart, that you, Mrs Collins, of all people, should fail to ascribe that virtue to me." The tirade ended in his withdrawing to his book-room and, after reflection, recollecting that he had been in the right all along: his daughter had in truth made a conquest of Mr Robert Pavey, and Mr Collins had been the first to see it. Thus vindicated, he took upon himself the credit for the attachment, and hence decided it to be an excellent thing; more, he exceeded his wife in considering it quite settled. The invitation to drink tea was accepted, to the relief of Mrs Collins.

She might have felt less relief, had she discussed in the interim with her husband Marcia's situation and discovered his revised opinion of it. As soon as he could make his way through the throngs in the Paveys' drawing-room, to the corner wherein Robert was standing solitary, Mr Collins proclaimed:

"Mr Robert – A good evening to you! What a delightful gathering this is! I assure you, I am empowered to express the gratitude of all my family for the excellent entertainment. Most significantly, of course, I speak for my daughter, whose modesty I see you are respecting, by not yet securing her attention. But modesty, on the part of a gentleman, can take on the appearance of reserve. Do not let any apprehension of my disapproval hold you back, my dear Mr Robert. I give you not only my permission, but my blessing."

"I thank you, sir," replied Robert much at a loss. "But I do not know what you mean?"

"Come, now," said Mr Collins in a jocular voice, "there is no need to dissemble. I admire frankness. I am being entirely frank with you myself, and I hope our relations will grow ever more amiable. I am sure that you are all that I could wish for as a son-in-law. I congratulate you."

Robert could not be frank enough to answer that he had no intention of acquiring Mr Collins as a father-in-law. Horrified by the mere notion, he excused himself with a meaningless murmur and withdrew. But as he began to wonder what could have suggested to Mr Collins that Robert had any idea of marrying his daughter, Robert began to wonder whether this notion were indeed as horrific. On the contrary, during a wakeful night, he pondered marriage with Miss Collins. It began to recommend itself to him.

Robert was, as his father had observed, always ready to fall in which his friends' wishes. Should Miss Collins wish to marry him, he would hate to disappoint her. He had a high regard for her character and valued her sympathy; in many ways he had come to depend upon her. And, supposing he were to become engaged, before Miss Webster and her captain appeared at Teverton, he would be safe. He would demonstrate to himself that he was cured of his hopeless passion and the world would not suspect that he had entertained it. The relief of this prospect rendered the idea of marriage with Miss Collins entirely excellent. On the very next morning at the breakfast-table, Robert informed his parents that he intended to ask Miss Collins for her hand.

Mr and Mrs Pavey, in their restrained fashion, offered no comment, beyond their good wishes for Robert's happiness. Since Robert's uncle and aunt were present, they felt it prudent not to exhibit their total surprise. Later, between themselves, they agreed that Miss Collins was a sensible, unassuming girl; having scarcely noticed her hitherto, they could say little more. "He could have chosen worse," said Mrs Pavey.

"And at any rate," added her husband," he has not, as you feared, fallen in love with any of the Miss Dallows."

THIRTEEN

Through the darkness of that same evening Robert rode out to Teverton Rectory and, when he was shown into the drawing-room, had the good fortune to find Mrs Collins and her daughter alone there. Marcia wondered that her mother said: "I will tell Mr Collins you are here," instead of bidding the servant or Marcia to do so; and when her mother had left the room, and Robert without delay made his proposal to her, it was wholly unexpected.

Robert was not vain enough to be surprised at her refusal, but his own disappointment surprised him. The refusal was so mild, that he underestimated its firmness. When she said that she did not feel their natures were fully compatible, he pointed out that in the closeness of matrimony they could become so. When she said that her own feelings for him were not of the necessary quality, he insisted that he would do all possible to earn and deserve her affection. He was certain by now that he had never longed for any other thing than to marry Miss Collins, and with every intention of renewing his application, he pressed her no more, but left his compliments to her father and mother, and rode away, planning busily to find ways of pleasing her.

Mrs Collins had detained her husband in his book-room for as long as possible; not till she heard hooves receding did she hurry back to the drawing-room, Mr Collins following, to learn the happy result of the interview. She was more disappointed almost than Robert had been, and more surprised.

"You refused him? But my dear Marcia, why?" And when Marcia supplied the same arguments that she had used with Robert, Mrs Collins shook her head. She could not help showing her displeasure. "I do not understand you at all."

Mr Collins added his remonstrations. He had understood, he said, that the engagement was a settled matter, and so, he was sure, had Mr Robert. Marcia's ingratitude and stubbornness were shocking to her father and added, he said with a hand to his brow, to his afflictions.

"I cannot see what you object to, in Robert Pavey," Mrs Collins said, persisting.

"I do not at all object to him, Mama."

"Then," put in Mr Collins, "you are perverse, as well as stubborn. Think less of yourself, and consider others, as is your duty. Connection with the Paveys would bring advantages to me and your mother, as well as to William in the course of his career. That family is one of the most respected in the district, and I wonder you can be insensible of the honour Mr Robert has accorded you. His father and mother will be displeased with you, and with all of us. We shall be punished for your selfishness."

Marcia had begun to cry miserably under the reproaches of both her father and her mother. "Now, my dear," said Mrs Collins pitying her, "do not distress yourself so. Let me take you to your room, and send for a warm drink." But in the privacy of Marcia's room, neither her tears nor her mother's persuasions ceased. Mrs Collins was not angry, but puzzled; she had been sure, on the evidence of her own eyes, that her daughter and Robert Pavey were mutually attracted, and she was still convinced of the suitability of the match. With patient firmness she repeated all the points in its favour.

"I know," admitted Marcia between sobs, "that all you say is right. I know I am being unreasonable and causing you sorrow." But even to her mother she could not confess what she held to be Robert's secret: his devotion to Miss Webster, whom no one would replace for him. Marcia was not too proud to accept second place; but she was hopeless of any merits in herself that could make up to him for his lost ideal.

Mrs Collins, recollecting, considered for a moment, then asked in a gentle voice: "Are you, my dear, I wonder, held back by any preference for Mr George Dallow?"

"No, indeed," said Marcia with decision. "You know that I at no time thought of Mr George ... in that way."

Mrs Collins believed her. "I see. I am glad of that. But I find you even more difficult to understand. But, please, do not cry any more. We shall leave the subject for the present. Calm yourself, and bathe your face, and go early to bed."

If Mrs Collins was prepared to leave the subject, Mr Collins was not. Yet another frustration, through no fault of his own, had fallen upon him and he lamented it tirelessly. For the succeeding two days, the atmosphere of the Rectory was exceedingly uncomfortable.

This was so for William, not because he involved himself in the issue of his sister's marrying Robert Pavey, on which his opinion was in any case not invited, but because in the meanwhile Mr Dallow had arrived home, closely followed by the contingent from Bath, and all at once Mr George had no time for Fitz. Mr George was glimpsed only as he sped past, riding with Walter or with Captain Godfrey. William's exclusion did little to reconcile him to the discomfort in his family.

"I wish," he remarked to Marcia, "that you would marry Robert."

"Why should you wish that, William?"

"Because then perhaps Father would stop being so disagreeable."

Marcia had expected no support from William, but that he himself should be disagreeable to her increased her isolation.

Robert called again at the Rectory, only to be intercepted by Mr Collins and to have his time taken up by Mr Collins's assurances that Marcia would at any moment become mindful of her duty and her true inclinations, and yield to her suitor. Mr Collins had persuaded himself that this was so, and spoke of the engagement as formed, adding only that there might be some short delay. In such terms he addressed Robert's father, whom he happened to meet in the town.

"Only my daughter's modesty, sir, hinders the fulfilment of your son's wishes. She shall soon be brought to a just estimation of her good fortune. I shall see to that; you may rely on me. I shall give her all the benefit of wise fatherly guidance and religious admonition. And my son William, whom you well know to be a right-judging young man, is giving his sister the best advice, from loyalty to his friend Mr Robert. My daughter will very soon be taught to know her own mind."

"I imagine," replied Mr Pavey, "that your daughter is not entirely ignorant of her own mind. We should leave the young people to decide the question between themselves. As for the right judgement of your son William," he added, bowing and turning away, "it has not been much evident in his work of late. My clerk complains often of his negligence. Good-day to you."

This encounter brought Mr Collins home in indignation. "I knew this would be so," he declared as soon as he entered the house. "Now Mr Pavey is beginning to turn against me; and what have I done to merit that? What have I done, to deserve children who betray me at every turn? Now Mr Pavey complains of your negligence at work, William. He —"

"I do not care what old Pavey complains of."

"Do not interrupt me. If Mr Pavey turns you off, what will become of you? You have no thought for your own interests. It is I, upon every occasion, who must intercede and exert myself, for no thanks —"

William shouted: "I do not thank you, for committing me for life to that dreary office."

"Do you dare shout at me, sir?" cried Mr Collins, flushing.

"I do dare," returned William, making his assertion self-evident at a pitch that must have been audible at the further side of the duckpond. Waiting for no response he ran up the stairs and slammed the door of his room.

"My love," said Mrs Collins as her husband drew breath to call William back, "I beg you to let him alone for the moment. He is overexcited."

Mr Collins was in some danger of falling into the same condition, in his outrage at this unprecedented rebellion. He obeyed his wife, in part because he could not immediately think of a method, consonant with dignity, of dealing with William. "You see, Marcia," he said, turning upon his daughter, "what trouble you bring upon us all. If William's career is destroyed, through your perversity, I hope you will have the grace given you to regret it."

"I shall have dinner served directly," said Mrs Collins.

William did not come to the table. At the end of the meal, Mrs Collins said: "I will take William a little soup upstairs, and see that he is ready to apologise —"

"You will take Master William nothing upstairs," Mr Collins told her with asperity. "Let him apologise before he eats any more of the food I provide for him. I will tolerate no more of his impertinence under my roof."

It appeared that Mr Collins spoke more truly than he knew. William did not appear for breakfast. Again, Mr Collins insisted that he be not approached, but Mrs Collins insisted in turn that William must not be allowed to be late at the office, and she went upstairs. She returned to say that William's bed had been undisturbed and that a quantity of his clothing was missing.

"Where can he be?" inquired Mr Collins.

"I do not know. He must have left the house during the night. He has run away. I was afraid of something like this."

"You did not warn me. I am the last to be told of my children's intentions. Why should he run away?"

Mrs Collins had no answer. She said only: "Where can he have gone? Marcia, do you know anything of this?"

Marcia shook her head, horrified by William's recklessness and afraid it would somehow be blamed on herself. And her father was announcing:

"My children have given me nothing but one worry and annoyance after another. How have I deserved it, that what should be the blessings of life turn in my case into afflictions?"

FOURTEEN

At the manor, the atmosphere during this time was considerably more cheerful than that of the Rectory. Mr Dallow's quest for antiquities had been rewarding, the family was joyful at being reunited and Captain Godfrey made a very favourable impression; his health, Mrs Dallow was glad to observe, appeared excellent; and Silvia was so happy with him.

George Dallow, relieved of the obligation of proposing marriage to Silvia, was more at ease with her and was affable in general. His father was gratified to discover how much work George had been putting into the estate and that he was genuinely interested; Mr Dallow's future expeditions might be undertaken without such qualms of conscience as he had hitherto, now and then, suffered; satisfaction prevailed.

The only person secretly troubled in mind was Corinna. While she agreed that Silvia was very happy with Thomas Godfrey, she did so with reservations, which at first she could not admit even to herself, since she was conscious of her own attraction towards Captain Godfrey – and in this, Mrs Forbes had been right: Thomas Godfrey had at the outset been attracted towards Corinna. If he chose to marry Silvia, then Corinna wished him well. If he had been tempted by Silvia's fortune, Corinna, spendthrift herself, could not blame him. If he had been over-influenced by his friend Henry Webster, he was more culpable. But if he loved Silvia for her beauty and sweetness, that was readily understandable. Corinna loved Silvia dearly, and felt, by now, more wordly-wise than her young cousin, as befitted her five years' seniority. She desired Silvia's true happiness, but herein lay the reservation. If Silvia loved Thomas Godfrey for his striking looks and gallantry, that was admissible. If she had been influenced by her brother Henry, her gentle nature made that excusable. But Corinna's acute perceptions warned her that, upon a deeper level, Silvia's whole heart was not awakened. Silvia's own temperament did not, ultimately, accord with that of Thomas Godfrey; she had, as it were, submitted to him rather than given herself. But why should this be? The answer did not come until they had been for a day or two back at Teverton. Then Silvia, in one of their private bed-time talks, for the two young ladies were now close friends, confided in Corinna that, just before they left Bath, Mrs Forbes in turn had confided in Silvia that she and Admiral Lawrence were hoping to marry, and to leave for Gibraltar together in the spring. "So she will be glad," Silvia ended, "that I am to be settled as well, and to set her free."

Much of Corinna's preplexity was resolved. There was an element of sacrifice in Silvia's accepting Thomas Godfrey, that Corinna had to admire, while she still wondered whether it would make for her cousin's deserved happiness. As she watched the betrothed pair together, she admitted that Thomas Godfrey stirred Silvia to unusual animation; but then, his irresistible manner would stir anyone; and, was such liveliness entirely natural to Silvia – was she perhaps, even unawarely, *trying* to be happy?

And Thomas Godfrey, affectionate and deferential towards Silvia, clearly adored her; but, when he was out riding, for instance, without her, did he not seem even more high-spirited – as if released? Corinna after serious thought came to a decision that involved some sacrifice on her own part: she would try to draw Captain Godfrey's attentions towards herself.

"It is against all principle," she reflected. "I have no desire to betray Silvia, and I am no wrecker of the lives of others. But I shall by that means test the strength of his attachment to Silvia, and if it does not stand the test, why, I shall be delivering Silvia from a marriage that would not suit her. She needs a steadfast and gentle husband. For that matter, Thomas Godfrey needs a wife more like myself. I should be more able to stand the rigours and shifts of army life, and I should not give way to him upon all questions; I have not Silvia's sweet nature. Well, I shall put temptation in the way of Thomas Godfrey, and resign myself to appearing a cruel flirt. In either outcome, I shall be the only sufferer."

The family at Teverton passed Christmas without additional company, glad to be together and isolated besides by a snowfall that kept them even from attending church on Christmas day. There was no want of entertainment within the Hall and in the communal gaiety Corinna could not at once further her designs. On the day after Christmas it was Jane, turning over the books of music on the pianoforte, who asked:

"Why has Robert not been to see us? I should like to hear him and Silvia sing together again."

"The weather has kept many of our friends away," said Mrs Dallow. "Not everyone has the constitution that can withstand it."

George, throwing down a fishing-line that he had been mending, threw aside too his festive air and said in a surly tone: "Have you not understood, that Robert is no friend of ours now? Nor have you heard that he has other affairs to occupy him? He is engaged to marry Miss Collins."

"Miss who? – Oh, the Rector's prim daughter. You surprise me."

George had been much surprised too by the news, as it travelled about the neighbourhood some time ago. He had taken no pains to verify the rumour, but had tried to put it out of his mind, mentioning it not even among the family.

The ironic, not to say ridiculous, situation had come about, that the positions of the two erstwhile friends were reversed. Robert had believed George to be engaged to the woman he himself loved, although that had not in truth been so; and now George believed Robert to be engaged to the young lady who, as a consequence of that, was taking on more value in his own eyes; although this latter engagement was not yet formed, in spite of the continued advocacy of Miss Collins's parents.

"Robert's being engaged, or the snow, should not keep him away," cried Philippa. "The snow is thawing already. Tomorrow, let us all walk into Fraxted, and call on the Paveys. I know they will like to meet Thomas."

The thaw was indeed begun, but, next day, Corinna proposed a walk in the fields, as more refreshing than a social visit. Mrs Dallow approved that, advising only that the girls wear their strongest boots and avoid the remaining drifts of now.

"There will be no drifts!" Philippa assured her, and the party set out, Corinna leading the way with Thomas Godfrey, on the pretext of pointing out to him some of the interesting features of the landscape. "We shall be able to ride again, now that the snow is gone," she said. "We must go as far as Marston Hill; the views from there are magnificent."

"Unfortunately, I have not much time remaining. I must

rejoin the regiment in six days from now."

"So soon!" cried Corinna startled. "I am so sorry," she added more smoothly. "– For Silvia's sake, I mean." Before Thomas could reply she turned her face from him, then noticed that they stood upon the edge of a considerable snowdrift lingering in a cleft of the hillside. "See, Philippa," she called, "how mistaken you were. Here is deep snow."

"We can turn back and take the lower path," suggested Philippa as she caught up with the leading couple. Corinna, impatient of any turning back, maintained that it would be possible to cross the drift; the surface was firm.

"No, allow me to disagree; the snow is thawing and soft," Thomas said.

"It may be too soft for your great weight, but I shall soon be across it," Corinna insisted, stepping boldly on to the snow. It gave way beneath her but, clutching at a far branch with one hand and dragging free her skirt with the other, she succeeded in achieving the opposite bank of the rill. Thomas, following her, sank in the snow to his waist, to the merriment of everyone. He struggled over to join her, while Jane, Philippa and Walter prudently made use of the branch that had served Corinna. Their passage softened and broke the snow more and Walter had to haul Jane out by the hands. George attempted a crossing higher up the slope, with little more success than Thomas, but he was over. Silvia, hesitating, was left behind. She called:

"I do not think I can face this. I shall go downhill, round the foot of the snowdrift, and catch up with you."

Thomas was still talking to Corinna and did not hear her; nor did anyone except Jane, who called back: "Very well. We shall meet you at the stile." So Silvia hurried down the field. The drift was longer than she had supposed. It ran past a clump of trees and almost down to the riverside. Rounding the clump of trees, she came face to face with Robert Pavey.

Robert, as Pavey and Son was still on Christmas holiday, had ridden out to walk beside the river, knowing that Marcia sometimes walked there. He had the excuse of seeking, should he meet her accidentally, news of her missing brother, of whom nothing had been heard, and of whom Robert preferred not to inquire at the Rectory. When, instead of Marcia, Miss Webster stood in his way, he could have believed it a trick of his vision. He stood speechless; but she roused him to the practical needs of the moment, addressing him first, in a breathless haste:

"Oh, Mr Pavey. Good-day. I am trying to avoid the snow – I said I would catch up with the others – but already I have lost sight of them. Do you know where the stile is? They said they would meet me there. But," as she looked downward, "I do not see how I can cross, even now." The melting snow had turned the rivulet at the foot of the drift into a formidable torrent that poured into the river.

"Miss Webster – How do you do? No, certainly you cannot step across here. I have jumped it myself but it is too much for you."

"Then I must turn back. Or will they be waiting for me? I wish I had been brave enough to step on to the snow, as the others did."

"Please let me help you," said Robert affected by her distress. "If you would allow me to lift you over the stream, I could then show you the way to the stile. They must mean the stile at the entry to Home Wood."

"I should be so grateful," cried Silvia. And, in a moment, he had lifted her in his arms and with one long stride had set her down on the path beyond the torrent. She smiled at him saying: "You are so kind. That is exactly how you saved me when I was a foolish little girl and afraid of the stepping-stones."

Robert was more than gratified by her recollection. He was emboldened to offer her his arm in climbing up the field, since the sodden grass was slippery. Accepting his arm, she said: "I have found another setting of 'The little red lark', in a book I have in Bath. I like it better than the setting in Mrs Ingle's book, but I did not think to bring the music with me."

She recollected their singing together, also. Robert hardly knew what he replied. He wished the ascent of the field were a hundred times longer, but very soon he was compelled to point out: "There is the stile, and there I see the others, waiting for you." Among the distant figures he could descry Walter, standing on the wall top and waving; and there too, he remembered, would be Captain Godfrey. Muttering some excuse about a meeting with a friend, he took a brief leave of Miss Webster and, not listening to her thanks, strode off again down the hill.

Later in that day, the same thought occurred to Robert and to Silvia: Each had, since they last met, become engaged to be married; neither had, when they met today, remembered to utter any congratulations. Both wondered how they could have been so remiss.

FIFTEEN

Corinna found her capture of Thomas Godfrey all too easy. There was, it must be admitted, some predisposition on both sides. When they returned from their walk, Mrs Dallow observed that Silvia was tired, and scolded the others for overtaxing her. Silvia was sent to bed with a posset, newly culled from a medical pamphlet, and Corinna took Captain Godfrey off for an inspection of her father's collection of Roman coins. This collection his family found inexpressibly uninteresting – as did Thomas Godfrey – but it provided him with an hour's *tête-à-tête* with Corinna. On the following day, when a riding party was practicable as the snow dwindled, Corinna contrived to become so much absorbed in a military tale of Captain Godfrey's, that she missed a turning in the woods and the two of them became separated from the others. By that evening, they were so much at one, that they were quarrelling over a game of cards. And on the day after that, neither of them could deny that they were in love. It took little encouragement from Corinna to cause Thomas to overcome his scruples and confess his feelings.

"I will tell you what we shall do," pronounced Corinna when she had confessed her own, and a brief interlude of bliss was arrested by the inevitable recognition of their quandary. Thomas awaited her instruction willingly; a girl of this determination and spirit provided a contrast to the gentle and docile Silvia; he would welcome any advice, on his extrication from his dishonourable position. "It would be best," Corinna explained, "to make a quick and total break. I do not want to hurt Silvia more than I must, or to have to argue the matter with my father and mother. Besides, we have so little time. We have decided what we are to do; let us do it, summarily. We shall simply run away, to Gretna."

Shocked by the suggestion, Thomas nevertheless came to agree. For all his valour, he was afraid to confront Silvia, although he believed Corinna when she told him he would be in effect setting Silvia free. Corinna undertook to write a letter to be left for Silvia, and Thomas penned a few remorseful lines upon his own account. The execution of their plan could not be delayed; already, only two days remained of Thomas's sojourn at Teverton. With three days in which to get himself to Scotland, married and back to his regiment, Thomas was as zealous as Corinna to set forth immediately. It was fortunate that the snow was gone. During that same night, so were the lovers.

The elopement threw the household of Teverton into a consternation that can be imagined. No one had suspected Corinna to be capable of such wickedness. Impulsive and self-willed she might be, but she was high-principled, open, and, everyone knew, had a great affection for Silvia. The principles of Captain Godfrey became suspect; those who had been with him in Bath now confessed that they had always thought him a flirt. Not that this exonerated Corinna; all agreed that she was not a natural victim for however fascinating a seducer. There was no thought, at any rate, of stopping the marriage; Mr Dallow tacitly admitted that, were he to set off post to Scotland and overtake his daughter, he would have little influence over her, were her mind made up; and Corinna's, before she acted, always was.

None of this discussion, naturally, took place in the presence of Silvia, who was, as naturally, everyone's primary concern. The composure with which she bore her desertion commanded admiration. She was pale and quiet, but if she wept it was in secret, and she uttered no reproach of either her fiancé or her cousin. "Corinna has written me a very kind letter," she said. "I am sure she does not wish to hurt me, and she feels all may be in the end for the best."

"She chooses a very strange way of not hurting you," exclaimed Mrs Dallow, who was curious to read that letter of Corinna's but, as Silvia did not offer it, had to puzzle out for herself her daughter's motives, meanwhile searching the stillroom for a restorative for Silvia.

Silvia, reading the letter, was herself still puzzled. Vanity should have been wounded, that another had stolen her suitor's affections, but Silvia was deficient in vanity. Throughout, she had not considered herself worthy of Thomas Godfrey. To read, in Corinna's letter, that Corinna considered it the other way about astonished her. She could not ascribe insincerity to Corinna and true affection showed in the letter's every line. That Thomas Godfrey should prove inconstant was a grief to Silvia as much upon Corinna's account as upon her own, when she looked ahead in imagination at the length of years. It did not much surprise Silvia – for from what her brother Henry said, military men were often impetuous and fickle – but could Corinna be happy with him? And, worst, would Corinna be separated by her misdeed from her own family?

But Jane and Philippa, when they felt it proper to discuss the question with Silvia, having permitted her time to recover from her initial shock, consoled her. "You will see, all will be forgiven. Our father and mother are angry for the moment, but Corinna will soon win her way back. She cannot mean to lose us. And, you know, no one thought any harm of Captain Godfrey, until this escapade. He is so well-looking and charming, no one could long withstand him. And if he is inclined to let his affections wander again, he will get short shrift from Corinna. She will not have entered into this marriage without knowing pretty well what she is about. She will have him received again at Teverton, though not, of course, while you are with us.''

"But I do not know that I should mind it, were I to meet ... him again,'' said Silvia.

"There – You see! You are a noble creature, Silvia.''

They admired their cousin's fortitude and, were it not for the harm caused to her, would have admired their sister's exploit too. Everyone, solicitous for Silvia, drew her closer into the family circle and she readily agreed to remain at Teverton for the present. Writing to Mrs Forbes, she made as light as she could of Captain Godfrey's defection and made much of the kindness of the Dallows to her. She wrote thus, in order to reassure Mrs Forbes, and made it sound, with this in view, almost as if she were relieved to be freed from her engagement. As she read over her letter, she began to wonder whether this were not indeed so. At this juncture, she was not unwilling to make Teverton her permanent home; she need not be a hindrance to Mrs Forbes's own plans.

In the same vein, Silvia wrote to her brother Henry, since he would otherwise be capable of calling out his friend to avenge the slight to his sister. Henry had fully intended to do so, as soon as Thomas and his bride arrived at the regimental quarters, whither the news of their elopement had preceded them, as it happened, by way of a brother officer who had passed them at a coaching inn on his own way south. When Silvia's letter reached Henry, it was fortunately just ahead of the advent of Captain and Mrs Godfrey, to Henry's relief. He was fond of Corinna and had no wish to contribute to the happiness of her married life by putting a bullet through her husband's heart at its outset. He was not able to make himself less friendly towards Godfrey either, especially when Corinna's persuasions had been added to the emollient effect of Silvia's letter.

From the regimental quarters, Corinna wrote to her parents, begging their forgiveness, proclaiming her happiness, and adding a list of her books and clothes that she wished her sisters would pack and send to her. Mr Dallow was already preparing for a journey to North Africa; Mrs Dallow was persuaded that Silvia's health had not suffered under her disappointment; in so short a time, the situation was already on the mend. Mr Dallow went so far as to mention to Mrs Dallow that Silvia was now free again to marry George; but Mrs Dallow recommended that more time for recovery be let pass, before the suggestion be made to George.

George, who had anticipated the suggestion, kept himself busily occupied at a distance from his cousin. He pitied her, but, now that a broken heart was added to her other attributes, found himself even more awkward in her presence.

The news of Miss Dallow's elopement had inevitably travelled fast through the countryside. It was a matter of indifference to the Dallows that they should be gossiped about; nor did they need to recount their affairs at large. There was still little communication between the manor and the town; rumour had to be self-perpetuating: Miss Webster was pining away, Mr George Dallow was to shoot Captain Godfrey, Miss Dallow was to have her name struck from the family Bible; this last item arose, it might be admitted, solely from a suggestion of Mr Collins's when

he was apprised of Miss Dallow's offence. Many of the
citizens and countryfolk found the whole tale diverting, but
Robert Pavey, pitying Miss Webster perhaps more than
anyone, would have given anything not to be at a distance
from her. Since their meeting by the river he had made a
renewed effort to put her out of his mind, but when he
heard that she had been abandoned by Captain Godfrey,
compassion and alarm overcame resolution. From his office
window he gazed in vain, seeing no one from Teverton,
from manor or Rectory. Marcia, too, had for some time
past avoided the sight-lines of that window – as she had,
since she remembered telling Robert that she liked to walk
by the river, denied herself that region also.

But, on a Monday, Robert perceived one of the servants
from the Rectory, crossing the street towards the door of
Pavey and Son. Within a minute, a note was delivered to
Robert's desk. When he saw that it was signed by Miss
Collins, he scanned it in haste.

"Dear Mr Pavey," she had written. "I do not know what
reports have reached you, but I am sure you will be glad to
hear that Miss Webster attended church yesterday with her
friends. She was in good health and very fair spirits. She
told me that she is to remain some while at Teverton. She
spoke to me with good feeling of her cousin's marriage.
Yours ..."

Robert was in a moment out in the street in pursuit of the
servant. He ran up and down until he caught sight of the
man above the market cross; hallooing wildly, Robert
gained his attention and, running up, asked whether Miss
Collins were in the town.

"Yes, sir. She is gone to the chandler's. I am to wait with
the chaise behind the market hall."

At that out-of-the-way meeting-place, Robert, the
servant and Marcia arrived simultaneously. Marcia looked

disconcerted and would have drawn back, but Robert, her note still in his hand, cried:

"Wait – I must speak to you. I thank you for your note –"

"I did not mean to meet you. Please forgive its presumption –"

"Why should you call it so? I am more thankful than I can say, for your kind thought."

"I imagined you might be anxious," explained Marcia in blushing confusion, "but it was officious of me to imply that – That I was aware of your particular concern for ... for the lady I mentioned –"

"But indeed I have been most terribly concerned for her, and your note gives me great comfort." Then it was Robert's turn to blush, as he recollected the state of affairs between Miss Collins and himself. In his contrition and shame, he seized her hand. "I am sure you have known," he said, "all along – You, alone, have been the witness of my secret, and I must beg you to forgive me for trespassing on your sympathy – And, please believe me, there has been no insincerity in any of my professions to you. Be assured of my true affection – The other is but a foolish dream – I hardly know what I am saying. You have been my only friend and comfort, and I could not bear to have you lost to me –"

The servant had turned away, to make himself noisily busy with the horse's harness, and Marcia had recovered some of her self-possession. "My friendship, you can be certain you will never lose," she told Robert. "And, if you remember, I have refused this long while to enter into any closer bond with you. You need have no fear of showing bad faith."

"But that is, inevitably, what this tumult of my feelings does show. You must think me two-faced, and stupid besides, as well as weak-minded to give way to romantic fantasy. Of that, I truly felt that my attachment to yourself had cured me. But you suspected it had not, and your tolerance and generosity of spirit put me to shame."

Marcia retrieved her hand and said in a more prosaic tone: "Why should you speak of romantic fantasy? I can well understand your admiration of – the young lady. She appeared lost to you, but now, surely, she is free once more?"

"She may be unattached," said Robert, heavily despondent, "but I could have no hope of – Consider her circumstances, and mine."

"Circumstances are but circumstances, when hearts are involved," stated Marcia with an authority surprising to herself, but evoked by Robert's despondency. "Do not be so hopeless. She is to be here for some while. She may even remain to live here. Who knows what may happen?"

Robert shook his head, but her encouragement soothed him. "You are too good to me. I must, in view of my admission, forfeit all hope of your accepting me. I wish it could have been otherwise. But your forgiveness, and the promise of your friendship, are strong supports. I thank you again, a thousand times, for your note, and its reassuring contents. But why," he added, rousing himself and looking round, "am I detaining you here over my troubles, when you have so many of your own?"

"The final decision, that you do not wish me to marry you, will relieve me of one of my troubles," said Marcia half smiling.

"Then I am glad. But – I dare hardly ask – what is the news of your brother?"

"There, our trouble remains," said Marcia, sighing. "We have heard nothing, since your father so kindly traced him to London."

It was Mr Pavey who had made all the effort that had

been made, to find William Collins. On the morning of William's failure to appear at the family breakfast-table it had happened that the observant Mrs Pavey, parting her curtains early, had seen Mr William, a travelling-bag in his hand, embarking on the first London stage. She had mentioned it to her husband, who, merely annoyed by such an unorthodox departure, had sent to Teverton Rectory for an explanation of it. None was forthcoming from the Rector, who wrote a note of flowery apology; but the Rectory servants told Mr Pavey's that Mr William was run away, that there had been a great quarrel with his father, that no one knew where he was gone and that his mother and sister were in a fright about him. Concerned for Mrs Collins, Mr Pavey had presumed to inquire at the coach office and, having occasion next day to travel himself to London, had pursued his inquiries at the coach office there. But no one notices a young man with a travelling-bag; William Collins's further destination remained unknown. He was believed to have no money; his own father meanwhile did nothing to assuage the anxiety of his wife and daughter by lamenting the disgrace William would bring upon them all when he was found roaming London destitute.

"I do hope he will soon be back," Robert now said to Marcia. "Or that he will communicate with you. Do you not know of any friends he might have gone to?"

"We have tried, and thought, and come up with nothing."

"It occurs to me now," said Robert suddenly, "that Fitz was, before he left, on close terms with George. George Dallow, you know. Your brother could well have confided his plans to George – or George might well have put Fitz up to any notion, and kept quiet about it."

"I believe you could be right," cried Marcia. "Why did I

not think of that? William was guided by Mr George in everything, and would have asked his advice, before he set out on such an adventure. Oh, would you please, Mr Pavey, ask Mr George what he knows?"

"I? No, I am afraid that would not achieve any result. George would divulge no secrets to me nowadays." Nor was Robert, for other reasons, disposed to approach Teverton Hall. "Your father will ask him. George will hardly refuse a request from a father, and his Rector."

"I will speak to my father, then. I thank you so much for the idea. It is kind of you to concern yourself with my worries —"

Robert said with warmth: "My kindness is nothing, compared with yours towards me." They parted on the friendliest terms.

SIXTEEN

Mr Collins, when Marcia approached him, declared that he had no intention of advertising his son's rebellious conduct by going cap-in-hand to Mr George Dallow or to anyone else. Marcia, however, still felt Robert's idea worth pursuit. She must do all she could to discover what had become of William, for his sake and her mother's, as well as for her own. But who would help her? As she pondered it, it became evident that she would have to appeal herself to George Dallow.

That afternoon, as dusk drew in, George rode home into the stable yard. The stable-boy who had been waiting for him came out with a lantern, whose light was sufficient to show a figure, also waiting, in the yard corner. "Miss Collins!" exclaimed George, much surprised.

She moved forward. "Excuse me – I knew I might find you alone here – I did not wish to come to the house. My father – That is, I do not want anyone to know that I came."

"You will not come indoors?" said George dismounting and throwing the reins to the boy. "Come at least into the harness room; there is a fire. Now," as he pushed open the door for her, "to what do I owe this unexpected honour?" Pleasantly tired, yet exhilarated, by his ride in the cold air, he was not sorry to delay his own return to the house.

"It is on account of my brother – I wondered – Could you tell me anything of him? Where he is gone, where I can find him?"

"Your brother? Oh yes; someone told me, of course. Fitz has run away, like my sister. It seems all the fashion. I cannot say that I blame him."

"I think you would, if you knew the anxiety he has brought upon my mother," said Marcia with some sharpness.

"I suppose you are anxious too," conceded George. He drew up a stool beside the hearth for Marcia, but she remained standing, lifting her shawl back from her shoulders in the heat of the fire. "But why should you ask me about him?"

"I cannot think of anyone else in whom he might have confided his plans."

"He did not confide any plans in me. I am afraid I can be of no help."

"He did not give you any hint? You are not keeping a secret from me?"

"If I were, do you imagine I would betray it?"

Marcia considered that, frowning. "I imagine you are honourable in guarding secrets. But I hope that you would be kind enough to give some indication at least that he is safe, for my mother's sake."

"For your sake, I would give any number of indications; unfortunately I have none to give," said George, regarding her not unsympathetically. In her nervousness, her cheeks reddened by the fire, she was animated to prettiness; he admired the sharpness with which she had spoken to him. "Naturally you are worried, but I see no great cause for it. Fitz is a strong and fairly clever young man and, if he is run away to sea or some such nonsense, should survive."

"I hope so. But why does he not at the least write to my

mother? – I need not trouble you further, however. I am sorry you know nothing."

"Well, I am sorry too. – Wait; I have an idea. Robert should know more of Fitz than I; Robert Pavey, you know – They worked together in that office every day. – But, fool that I am, you must already have consulted Robert. I forgot, for the moment, that you are engaged to be married to him."

"I am not engaged to be married to Robert Pavey," said Marcia with some emphasis.

"You are not?"

George was for some moments astonished, but as he absorbed her meaning, a most surprising pleasure struck him, and, in the informality, the virtual intimacy, of this interview, he expressed without reflection or delicacy the idea that sprang to his mind:

"Then you must marry me!"

In that impulse, all was plain to him: He would have this enchanting and intelligent girl for his own, he would be delivered from Silvia, he would be happy ever after.

His impulse had, on Marcia, the effect of a stab to the heart. She was standing closer to Mr George that she had realised, gazing into his face; now she stepped back, her eyes angrily sparkling.

"I am not to be mocked, sir!" she cried, and, snatching her shawl close about her, she turned and hurried from the room before George could begin:

"I am not mocking – Do not go – Miss Collins, I beg you –"

She was gone. He hurried after her, calling: "Wait – It is dark, you will not find your way –" Her flight had been so rapid that he was afraid now for her safety. She was not to be seen; George shouted to the stable-boy to run after her with his lantern, forced to admit that his own escort would be totally unacceptable.

"Fool that I am," he muttered to himself, without understanding what had gone awry; he had spoken precipitately, but why had she been so much offended?

The boy needed to run to catch up with Marcia and he received no thanks for his guidance. Marcia was blinded by tears rather than by the darkness and did not notice the boy's presence. She ran down the lane not caring whether she fell or not, and at home, ran up to her room, to let her horror and misery have vent in private. She had known that George Dallow could be thoughtless – even inconsiderate – but she had not believed him capable of cruelty. The feeling for him that she had for so long suppressed now broke forth with the greater violence for its having been denied. She felt as if he had seized the very heart from her body and held it up to derision. Naturally, she had never thought of George Dallow's marrying her; then why should he make a joke of it? In her present desolation, it could not occur to her that George was not aware of her feeling for him; nothing, indeed, could occur to her except that she was scorned and wished to die. She wept until she was exhausted, but still the pain persisted. She could not go down to dinner.

Mrs Collins, forbidden to do so by her husband, came up to see what ailed Marcia and was appalled to find her in such a state. She could not persuade Marcia to reveal its cause and was afraid to press for explanations. She had never known her rational daughter so distraught.

"My dear, you will make yourself ill, if you do not try to be calmer. You have been under a severe strain. I know that your father, in his anxiety for your welfare, sometimes insists on his point of view – And if I too have been too insistent, I am very sorry. I am sure that if Mr Robert Pavey –"

Marcia interrupted in a broken voice: "There is nothing

... Mr Robert Pavey and I have agreed ... We are friends –"

"It is nothing to do with Robert Pavey, that you are so much upset? Then ...?"

Marcia grew slowly quieter. She lay still for a moment, and then said with an attempt at her normal manner: "I am sorry to be so ... foolish. It is nothing, and it is over now."

Mrs Collins was convinced that this was not 'nothing', but she tried to help Marcia regain her spirits by distracting her. "I wonder if it would do you good, to have a little change. Would you not like to go away, even for a few days, and rest? You remember that they asked you to visit them in Derbyshire, and that your aunt Maria invited you –"

"Oh, no, Mama, I could not leave you. Not until we have some news of William."

"If that is all," said Mrs Collins fancying that Marcia had been tempted by her suggestion, "You need not go as far as the north; any news of William could quickly be sent on to Hertfordshire. Would you not like to see them, and your grandmother?" Mrs Collins would very much have liked to visit her family herself; she wondered, too, whether a separation from Robert Pavey might not soften Marcia's heart even now towards him. And Marcia herself longed for nothing more than to escape from Teverton, whithersoever. She said that she would be glad to go to Aunt Maria's, were that possible, and her mother said with resolution:

"Then I shall write to Maria, this evening, and send it to the post early tomorrow. I should in any case write, for I have not heard from her for several weeks now, and am beginning to be anxious. Now, let me help you to bed, and you must sleep; I believe you are tired out."

Mrs Collins had not written to her sister, hoping that she would soon have news of William to despatch; she did not

want to confess his unexplained absence to anyone, until
compelled. She was, however, also worried that she had not
heard from Maria, and hoped that no trouble on Maria's
side had similarly prevented her from writing.

In the nature of such things, a letter from Maria arrived
on the next morning, when Mrs Collins's to her was sealed
but not yet sent. Mrs Collins had not been mistaken: Maria
explained that she had not written until the doctors
pronounced her younger daughter, Susan, to be free from a
threatened affection of the lungs, but now that Susan was
safe, her mother wrote cheerfully and at length of local
affairs:

"The rains flooded the road above the ford," wrote
Maria, "and the brewer's dray was caught up to the axles. I
am glad William is quite recovered from the tumble off his
horse. I met him in Meryton yesterday and he said his
shoulder is only a little stiff. They are ploughing the east
meadow at Longbourn, but of course he will be telling you
about everything there himself. I also met Mr Tucker, who
told me Miss Dodd is to be married at last, to ..."

But whom Miss Dodd was to marry, Mrs Collins had not
the slightest curiosity to know. She reread the preceding
lines, and read them again, slow to take in their import.
William was alive. He had gone to Longbourn – to that
estate in Hertfordshire, so long extolled as the Collins
inheritance. Maria believed that William's mother knew it
and that William was in correspondence with Teverton.

As soon as she had understood, Mrs Collins hastened to
her husband's book room with the letter. "My dear," she
cried, breaking in upon him, "here is excellent news. Let us
thank heaven, William is safe. He is at Longbourn – has
been, probably, since he left here. What could be more
natural? Why did we not guess? Here is a letter from Maria
– You shall see for yourself –"

Mr Collins studied the letter for some time. "I am obliged to agree with you," he said, raising his head at last, with an expression of displeasure. "William is at Longbourn. What, am I to understand, is he about? Must I suppose that my cousin has given him hospitality, has taken him in, knowing that he has run away from the paternal home in flagrant defiance of all duty and affection?"

"It may be that William did not tell your cousin the circumstances of his leaving home. He does not appear to have told Maria –"

"The more shame on him. He is deceitful, in that case, as well as rebellious. I shall write to my cousin forthwith."

"I hope, Mr Collins, that you will not set him against William –"

"I hope, my dear, that you will not dare dictate to me what I must say." Gesturing to his wife to leave him, he took up his pen. Mrs Collins hurried to find Marcia, and to share her happiness at William's having suffered nothing worse than a fall from horseback. The relief did a little to raise Marcia's spirits.

"And when you go to Maria's," Mrs Collins added, "you can see William, and write to tell me how he does."

But, at the breakfast-table, it was made plain that Marcia was not to be allowed to visit her aunt. Mr Collins forbade it absolutely. "I will not have my children forsaking and defying me. You must recollect your duty, Marcia, the more as William fails to. You will not leave this house. Except," he appended, "in order to be joined in the holy state of matrimony, which is also a duty, obstinate and insolent as you are in refusing to fulfil it."

He withdrew to his book-room to make a fair copy of the letter to his cousin, which finally ran:

"My dear Sir: It has come to my knowledge, by indirect means, that my son William is residing in your house. No doubt you are aware that he quitted the paternal roof without permission, without stating his destination, and at a cost of considerable anxiety to his family. I must warn you that he is, in spite of the best of example and education, turned out insolent, idle and intransigent. My disappointment in him has added to the many I have had to bear, and of which it is not necessary to remind you. It is your Christian duty to speed the prodigal back to his home, where I shall perform my paternal duty of just chastisement. Cast out, I adjure you, the viper from your bosom, before he turns again and rends you, as he has me. I do not ask any gratitude for this advice, but offer it humbly, in your own best interests. Yours most respectfully, William Collins."

As this literary composition so absorbed him, Mrs Collins felt that she could venture not only to go into Fraxted on some errands, but to take Marcia with her. The air would do Marcia good and the stricture that she be confined to the house could be taken, one hoped, figuratively. As they drove, they spoke cheerfully of William, and it was Marcia who said: "Mama, I think we should call at the Paveys', and tell them that we have heard of William. Mr Pavey was so kind in seeking him, and Mrs Pavey so concerned for us."

"By all means," assented Mrs Collins, surprised nevertheless, since she had noticed how sedulously Marcia had avoided not only the Paveys but their part of the town, of late. What was more, Marcia went on, tranquilly: "If you wish, I will call there, while you go to Jarrolds', for I know you want to be early there. Mr Robert will be glad to know, too, that William is discovered."

When they reached the market square, Marcia left her mother and was shown up into Mrs Pavey's drawing-room. Mrs Pavey was as glad as had been expected, to know that

William was located. "Wait," she cried, "I shall send for Robert, and you may tell him at the same time." But she could not wait; Marcia had to explain about her aunt's letter. As Robert was still not come up from the office, Mrs Pavey added to her expressions of relief and pleasure: "I am glad to see you, Miss Collins, alone for a moment, because Robert has given us to understand that all is over between you. I hardly know what to say to that; I am sorry for it; but he tells us that all was arranged in an amicable way – that is, there are no hearts broken over it?"

"No, indeed, ma'am. Mr Robert and I have agreed to remain good friends," said Marcia, without embarrassment, as Mrs Pavey was pleased to notice.

"Well, as a mother, of course I do not expect you will find another such young man as my son. But nor do I expect him easily to find your equal, my dear. I was determined to make myself love you," she added with her unaffected candour, "and I have succeeded."

The topic of other partners to be sought by Robert and herself was threatening Marcia's composure, when Robert's step was heard in the corridor and his mother was quick to call: "Robert, you must hear what Miss Collins has to tell us of her brother!"

"From your voice," said Robert entering the room, "I gather that it is good news. Good day to you, Miss Collins – Fitz is found?" He came towards her, and listened to the story of the aunt's letter, with such a natural friendliness that his mother, looking from face to face, was able to persuade herself that no harm had been done on either side. She wondered at the resilience of the young; Robert had been in deep melancholy ever since he had formed his attachment to Miss Collins, yet look, Mrs Pavey told herself, at the pair of them now!

"My father has written to ask that William be sent

home," Marcia was saying.

"I should think William is better off where he is," Robert remarked. "I doubt that my own father would welcome him back, into the firm."

"Oh, Robert," exclaimed Mrs Pavey, "you know how forgiving your father's disposition is!"

"I do, but I wonder if Fitz's disposition would be inclined to take up work in the office again, were he sent home forcibly."

"It depends upon my father's cousin. I know nothing of him. He may take to William, and refuse my father's request," said Marcia, though with some doubt. She felt it unlikely that William, as he had recently behaved at home, could ingratiate himself elsewhere.

She made her farewells to Mrs Pavey and was conducted down the stairs by Robert, who in the vestibule thought to ask: "Did George, by the way, know anything of this plan of Fitz's? Did your father ask him?"

Unexpectedly, this question discountenanced Miss Collins. She was silent, blushing, then as rapidly turning pale. Catching her breath she said: "No – Well, he did not know – My father would not ... Yesterday, I – Please, do not ask me. I cannot speak of ... him."

"Of George Dallow?" asked Robert bewildered.

"I must go – Excuse me."

She was now in tears. Robert already had the door half opened and she slipped past him and down the steps without raising her head. He stood holding the door and looking after her, wondering and troubled.

SEVENTEEN

The neighbourhood was amazed to hear that Captain and Mrs Godfrey were to pay their wedding visit to Teverton Hall at the beginning of February. It was so like the Dallows, remarked the neighbourhood, to expect poor little Miss Webster to receive the man who had jilted her a mere few weeks ago. The neighbourhood was disappointed of strife and violence among the Dallows following the scandal, so resented their too swiftly restored harmony. So is family affection, among other things, disparaged when it flouts convention.

The Dallows had reckoned not with convention nor its flouting, but with Captain Godfrey's next leave from the regiment. Also, Mr Dallow was upon the eve of departure and wished to see Corinna before he went. Silvia had of course been considered; she had assured her cousins that she would not at all mind meeting Thomas Godfrey again.

"Well, my dear," said Mrs Dallow, "we shall make the whole occasion as happy as possible, and give a dinner or two, and a ball, so that you may not find winter in the country too dull. I am afraid you are missing Bath."

"I am not at all dull here. I do not miss Bath, especially in the winter. Only, I should very much like to see Mrs Forbes again, before she is married and gone abroad."

It then occurred to Mrs Dallow that Mrs Forbes should

be invited to Teverton when the Godfreys came. "They can travel together, you know. That will make it easier for her. And Henry must come, if he can have leave. – No, Silvia dear, you would not be troubling us! This is your own home now, and you must invite any guests you wish."

Mrs Forbes, who was anxious to know for herself how Silvia fared, accepted the invitation. So did Henry, who told Mrs Forbes he intended to bring with him a delightful friend of his called Richardson, who would be the very husband for Silvia. From this Mrs Forbes dissuaded him, but Henry determined that, once Mrs Forbes was in Gibraltar, he would see to it that his sister did not become a rustic old maid.

Silvia's guardians also did not intend her to be an old maid. When Mr Dallow's patience had extended itself to the abnormal length of three weeks, he mentioned to his eldest son that Silvia might soon welcome consolation, in the form of another suitor for her hand. "I would like to see her happy again, before I go away," he explained. Legal and estate affairs could await Mr Dallow's convenience, but he was fond of Silvia and, when his affections were involved, saw no reason for delay.

"I will not propose marriage to Silvia," George declared.

"I am sorry to hear that. You are of an age to marry, and should be thinking of it. And Silvia is in every way to be recommended."

"I am thinking of marriage," retorted George in an irritable tone. "And I dare say Silvia would not have me, were I to ask."

Mr Dallow received both these statements with some surprise. He was glad that George was prepared for matrimony; it indicated that the boy was growing in every way steadier and acquiring a sense of responsibility. It was unlike George, however, to suppose himself unacceptable to anyone. George had been used to display an unthinking conceit of himself that his father would have fancied indestructible.

"Why should Silvia not have you? You have every advantage, of birth, situation, appearance and – when you make the effort – manners."

"I thank you for your good opinion, sir, but I cannot depend on its being shared by others. In any event, I should not make Silvia happy, and will not marry her, and would be glad if you would take that as decided."

"Well, well, we shall see. If you wish to marry, there is no one else whom you have met who would suit you. Nor does Silvia see a variety of company here. Do not, then, let me hurry you, but I shall still hope that proximity may take effect."

George argued the point no further. He perceived that his father's mind was set, while his own was in some commotion. He had overstated the case in saying that he thought of marriage; he thought, often, of the rebuff he had received from Miss Collins on that subject. He had spoken impetuously, but had he deserved such anger? The blow to his self-esteem had been salutary; it was occasioned not so much by Miss Collins's refusing to take his proposal seriously, as by his own admission that he had made a fool of himself. Miss Collins's value was enhanced, in proportion as George's of himself fell. The unprecedented turmoil of George's mind had stirred even his heart; he was in a fair way to be in love.

Marcia could not have suspected such a response in him. She hoped only never to see him again, and the recovery of her spirits was not encouraged by an invitation for 'The Reverend William, Mrs and Miss Collins' to a ball at Teverton Hall on the third evening of February.

"Must we accept?" she ventured.

"I deplore it, that I must constantly remind you of your duty," said Mr Collins. "I myself anticipate no pleasure upon such an occasion, yet do you hear from me such plaints of selfish ill-humour? I am prepared to set aside my own wishes in order to gratify those of others, and I exhort you, Marcia, to imitate my example." He was frequently heard at present to proclaim that he expected no pleasure from his life. Persuaded at last that Marcia was not to marry Robert Pavey, he was dejected enough to suppose that she would receive no further offers, but would remain a charge upon his purse for ever, and frequently told her so. It was no mitigation of his misfortune, that he had evidently been relieved of the maintenance of his son. William had not been sent home from Hertfordshire. Mr Collins's cousin had written in reply to his letter:

"My dear Sir: I misunderstood the unexplained arrival of your prodigal viper, and took him to be another of your olive branches. He is being actively employed by my bailiff about the farm, and promises well. As the estate will, in I hope the very distant future, devolve upon him, he is usefully occupied. I find his company congenial and trust, to cite your own parable, that he may continue to share my husks. Yours, &c ..."

Further letters of remonstration from Mr Collins had elicited no answer; nor had William communicated with his family. Mrs Collins trusted, however, that her sister's letters would report anything of note that occurred at Longbourn, and she and Marcia agreed that William had adopted a wise course, however unkind his behaviour towards themselves. Mr Collins could not admit that William had showed wisdom, concealed as it was within disobedience to himself; it was less credible to him than it had been to Marcia, that William should recommend himself to the master of Longbourn, and a source of alarm, that William might in effect cut Mr Collins out of his inheritance by assuming authority in the estate. Mr Collins must purge his conscience of the sin of envy, by reminding himself that William deserved none of this apparent success, and William's underhand and base nature was another frequent topic of his father's dissertations at the family table.

Mrs Collins was overcoming her own disappointment at Marcia's final refusal of Robert Pavey, and wished Marcia too could regain some of her cheerfulness. She knew of nothing, apart from the question of Robert, which could account for Marcia's continued dejection. Trying to raise her daughter's spirits she said: "Well, we shall make you a new gown for the ball. And although I know your father will now, even less, let you go to Hertfordshire, how would you like to go to Derbyshire in the spring? It could somehow be arranged; I shall see to it. You know how glad our friends there would be to see you."

"I should like that very much," replied Marcia with no more than a polite enthusiasm. She took up the lilac sprigged muslin, wondering that she felt so much older and sadder than she had when – so recently – she stitched at its seams in preparation for the first ball at the manor. Now, again, she was leading her life of so few months ago, helping her mother with domestic and parish affairs, but missing William's presence. Occasionally she had some comfort from her new, sisterly, relationship with Robert Pavey; and she had recently formed another friendship that pleased her.

One mild day, as she was walking beside the river, no longer afraid that Robert Pavey might seek her there with matrimonial intentions, she met Miss Webster, walking alone. Miss Webster explained, with some bashfulness, that Jane and Philippa were gone riding, but that she herself was afraid of horses and preferred to walk; exercise, she added with a smile, being obligatory at the manor. Marcia, smiling too, said: "You may at any time consider yourself pre-engaged to walk with me, should you be in need of an escape from riding." And so, on several fine afternoons, Miss Webster called at the Rectory for Miss Collins. They talked of books, and gowns, and wild flowers, and each enjoyed the other's society. Early in their acquaintance, Miss Webster asked with diffidence:

"You must forgive me for putting a very impertinent question to you, but no one seems to be sure of it, and although it is no concern of mine, I wish to understand, in order to have true confidence between us: Are you, Miss Collins, engaged to marry Mr Robert Pavey?"

By now, Marcia was able to dismiss the question without embarrassment. "No, I am not. There was for a while the possibility, but we both agreed that it would not be suitable, and that we should be happier merely as friends."

Miss Webster blushed a little, but Marcia imagined it could have been from consciousness of her own forwardness. She wished she might have told Robert of Miss Webster's inquiry; she did not know why Robert made no approach to Miss Webster now that she, twice over, had been opportunely set free. Marcia had no idea of Miss Webster as an heiress, nor would Robert's professional discretion have admitted to Marcia that he had. When he heard that Miss Webster had been walking with Marcia, Robert exhibited a keen interest in the details of their excursion. He was enchanted to be told that Miss Webster had worn her white tippet, or that she had failed to identify an alder catkin. He was pleased, for Miss Collins, that she had made so delightful a friend. He knew that she was not happy, and wished to make her happier; he still suspected that in some way George Dallow had distressed her, but could not imagine what she had had to do with George, nor could he discover from his oblique inquiries, what George had done to her. He would have, in his championship of Miss Collins, surmised George to be capable of anything.

Silvia, during her walks with Miss Collins, liked to hear her speak of Robert Pavey and observed that Miss Collins did so with naturalness. She observed, too, that Miss Collins was less willing to speak of the Dallows, and that when Silvia's cousin George was mentioned, the subject could even suffer an abrupt change. At the manor, George had less tact than Robert in his obvious interest in the walks of the two young ladies:

"What did you talk about? Did she speak about me?"

"We did not mention you, I think. We spoke of everyday things," said Silvia.

"If she talks of me, you must tell me what she says."

"Indeed, George, I could not do so, supposing that she did."

George was not ready, this time, with a scathing reflection on the discretion of young ladies. He said, in a gloomy voice: "No, I dare say not."

Silvia wondered whether he were attracted to Miss Collins; and, if so, why he made no approach to her?

Thus matters stood, when on the first day in February Captain and Mrs Godfrey, with Mrs Forbes, and Henry Webster, arrived at Teverton Hall. Their reception was so tumultuous that Mrs Forbes at first did not wonder at Silvia's childhood terror of this family; but her own welcome was so kind and, as soon as Mrs Forbes had told Mrs Dallow that Silvia's health seemed the better for country air, Mrs Dallow herself was so cordial that Mrs Forbes felt herself at ease even in the tumult. This subsided, with the initial excitement; Silvia greeted Captain Godfrey with composure and the evening passed happily. Mrs Forbes had to find time for a confidential talk with Silvia, however, before she could rest. She went with Silvia to her room at bed-time.

"You truly are happy here – and do not mind it, that Captain Godfrey is come?" asked Mrs Forbes, accustomed to being frank with Silvia.

"Yes, I am happy," said Silvia, as frank with Mrs Forbes, the only person to whom she had been used to open her heart. "And now that I see Captain Godfrey again, I recognise that I would have been mistaken to marry."

"To marry Captain Godfrey, or to marry at all?" Mrs Forbes pursued, teasing. But Silvia considered this question with widened eyes.

"I have never thought of marrying anyone else."

"No, I believe not. You are young of your age, my dear. There will be time enough to find and marry someone other, whom you truly love. I do not believe you loved that young man; will you not confess it?"

Silvia was indeed young, for her years. She had conceived of marriage as not irrelevant to love, but rather as a duty transcending it. She thought the matter over, and said: "I suppose I did not. But is it possible, that one could marry for ... Well, for affection?"

"I am about to do exactly that."

"But it is different for you," said Silvia in all innocence. She felt that Mrs Forbes had all the qualities she herself lacked and could afford to bestow herself in the certainty of giving pleasure. "No one could love me –"

"I will not listen to such nonsense. I am afraid you have been more hurt by that scamp Godfrey that you are aware of. When you find a man you love, you will be surprised by the merits that bloom in you. Sometimes it works, in that fashion."

Silvia lowered her face, playing with the sash of her night-gown, and Mrs Forbes's acute perceptions followed the progress of the girl's thoughts: There is, she decided, someone to whom Silvia is drawn. She is afraid only to trust her own heart in its awakening. Who can this man be? There is not a great choice, here. I must be on the watch. I will not have Silvia hurt again.

She sent Silvia to bed, with no more discussion, and next day began her scrutiny of the persons around her, for which there was not much leisure, since everyone was occupied in preparations for the morrow's ball. Discounting Silvia's own brother and the discounted Captain Godfrey, the choice was limited indeed; there was only Walter, who was exactly as Mrs Forbes had known him in Bath and whose manners could not be imagined to resemble those of anything but a young brother; and there was the eldest brother, George, whom Mrs Forbes had not met before this. He seemed to her a very different character. Courteous to Mrs Forbes, he treated his family with a peremptory authority; what interested her in him was that, when he fancied himself unobserved, he would scowl to himself, like a man troubled in mind. He was not long unobserved by Mrs Forbes. Nor was Silvia, whose own eyes appeared to rest on George at times in mild puzzlement. It had occurred to Mrs Forbes, some time ago, that a marriage between Silvia and this heir to Teverton would be desirable. The idea now recurred. Upon the evidence, or lack of alternative evidence, it was taking on form.

Mrs Dallow had begun to direct the roasting and baking in the kitchens, but meanwhile insisted on showing Mrs Forbes her stillroom. It was not difficult for Mrs Forbes, after admiring the tidy arrangement and health-giving properties of the herbs, to lead the conversation to Mrs Dallow's family and to remark that it must be a comfort to her that her eldest son was now of an age to be responsible for the estate during his father's absences.

"Yes, Mr Dallow is very pleased with George. We did not think he would grow so steady, you know. He has done very well with the tenants, seeing to repairs, and has a new sawmill building. He admits to his father that he is thinking of marriage, if to no one in particular as yet. His father and I did hope, you know, that he might marry Silvia, but he says he will not. We should have liked that; we love her so."

"Why should he not wish to marry Silvia?"

"Between us, my dear Mrs Forbes, it could be merely that his father put the suggestion to him. You know how young people prefer to make up their own minds, without advice. But please do not tell Mr Dallow my opinion. Do you see this coriander I sent for from a special garden in Cornwall ..."

So, reflected Mrs Forbes, George refused to marry Silvia under paternal guidance. George was, nonetheless, displaying to her sharp eye many of the symptoms of a man in love, and not happily so. During the day he was for the most part out of doors about his business. As it was fine, Mrs Dallow later collected the ladies of the household and led them out for their daily administration of fresh air; they walked to the village, since Mrs Forbes expressed a desire to see it, and returned by the churchyard so that she might admire its yew trees. When they turned the corner of the wall towards the duck-pond, Silvia caught Mrs Forbes's arm saying:

"There is my friend Miss Collins. I should so much like you to meet her." A young girl, emerging from an adjacent gateway, approached in response to Silvia's call and was introduced. She seemed to Mrs Forbes a modest, intelligent girl and all that had been described in Silvia's letters. Philippa said:

"You will meet again tomorrow. You are coming to our ball, are you not, Miss Collins?"

Miss Collins appeared to make some effort to reply, that she would be happy to come to the ball. As she was speaking, the sound of hooves caused everyone to glance round and move to the roadside. George Dallow in his curricle came swiftly round the bend of the road. Seeing the group, he slowed his horse, then, suddenly scowling and with the briefest salute of his whip, he flicked the reins and sped off up the lane towards the manor.

"How ill-mannered of George, not to stop and speak," his mother complained. "It might have occurred to him, at the least, that Mrs Forbes would be tired, and glad of a ride home. I apologise for him, Mrs Forbes. Let us hope his head was full of his business."

It may have been, but Mrs Forbes knew that he had intended to stop, until his eye had fallen on – Silvia? She looked to Silvia, who was intent on arranging the folds of her cloak and would not look up. As they walked up the lane, she drew Silvia a little aside to ask:

"Is Mr George often as unmannerly as he was just now?"

Silvia shook her head, her brow puckered. "Sometimes I do not understand Geroge at all."

"In what way, my dear?"

After hesitation, Silvia said: "I would rather not speak of it."

Denied for once Silvia's confidence – she did not doubt that it was Silvia's; Miss Collins had been, to her, a background figure in the encounter – Mrs Forbes was provoked into some annoyance with George. This, upon recollection, she admitted to be unjust. The young man was clearly not happy, and could need help, which Mrs Forbes, officious as it might be, would endeavour to give. She could not let herself forget that she had allowed herself to be mistaken over Silvia's feelings for Captain Godfrey. If Silvia, this time, were reticent, that could indicate a deeper feeling, which Mrs Forbes would not place at hazard.

By the time Mrs Forbes had the opportunity of speaking to George, her annoyance was softened and she was coming to pity him. At the dinner-table, his air of sad preoccupation made her imagine that some private reason prevented his approaching Silvia; persuasion might reveal it. If there were any impediment, it would be better revealed, and an end made to this suspense between the two cousins. In the drawing-room, all the young people were running too and fro, arguing the placement of furniture and flowers for tomorrow's party, but George sat alone on a far sofa, showing so little interest in the matter that it was permissible for Mrs Forbes to approach saying:

"You are not fond of dances, Mr George? You look as if you find all this disturbance tedious." She seated herself beside him and he roused himself to reply:

"I believe the disturbance is what my sisters enjoy. If they were to leave the arrangements to me, all would be settled in a half hour."

"But, to them, the planning of a pleasure is a large part of it."

"I do not know; I have not the patience to make plans."

"You will have to do so, though, in your work on the estate? Not everything there can be done upon impulse?"

"I do not know about impulse; but I like to decide things as fast as I can."

Pleased to find him ready for conversation, she pursued: "You are quick to make up your mind? That is valuable. Provided, of course, that you make the right decision, and stand by it. Some people who make decisions quickly are as quick to revoke them."

"That, I should call a sign of weakness."

"Or it could show courage, to admit a mistake?"

George sighed. "Yes; ladies can see the other side of every question. My sisters, as you observe, see so many sides to the disposition of the pianoforte, that I do not doubt it will finish up exactly where it stood when the discussion began."

Now that he had introduced the topic of ladies, Mrs Forbes persisted: "Women, you think, are more likely than men to change their minds? And men more likely to hold to a decision, though they may regret it?"

"I do not know. I do not know much about women. Indeed," he went on, unable to resist her sympathetic interest, "I suppose that when a woman does make up her mind, she can be harder to shift than any man. Or, I would have no idea of how to set about retrieving a position, when a woman had put me at a disadvantage. Or when," he added in gloomy candour, "I had so put myself, in regard to her."

Mrs Forbes, studying her folded hands, said gently: "You have some particular young lady in your thoughts."

"I suppose that is not hard to guess." He struggled against the impulse to confide in this amiable, perceptive and kind lady who was, best of all, a stranger; then, as was usual with George, the impulse prevailed. "I have, I may as well admit, been too impetuous in – in a personal matter, and given a wrong impression. I have forfeited the respect of someone whose good opinion I should highly value, and I can see no way of regaining it. In truth, I do not deserve to."

"But, if you confess yourself at fault, you can be forgiven – by any person who had a regard for you?"

"Well, but she has not."

"Are you sure of that? I should not agree."

George asked bluntly: "What do you know about it?"

"Little, I admit. I have seen the two of you together, if only for a short time, and I am vigilant."

"And what did your vigilance yield?" asked George, attempting scorn.

"Naturally, I cannot speak for the young lady. I am giving you only the results of my observations; and they are, that you should revoke your decisions, correct your impetuousness, cease to be so despondent, confess your errors and hope for a reward in the lady's more than forgiving you."

"You think she might?" said George, encouraged.

"If she does not, and if the situation is now as hopeless as you say, I do not see what either of you can lose."

"You are right," exclaimed George. "It cannot make matters worse, whatever my blundering. By G –, excuse me, ma'am – I will do it. I will try."

Mrs Forbes was about to wish him every success, when Henry Webster came up to them crying: "George, I am sorry to interrupt this solemn conference, but at what time in the morning may we have the men in to move the heavier furniture?"

George was compelled to give his attention to the general business, but he did so with a cheerfulness that told Mrs Forbes that her interference, whatever its outcome, had for the moment afforded him some relief.

EIGHTEEN

George Dallow might regret his own impetuosity, but he could not restrain it. He must see Miss Collins at once, if only to prove Mrs Forbes wrong. Mrs Forbes must be a deuced clever woman, to infer from that passing encounter at the Rectory gates what Miss Collins's feeling for George might be. His trouble was that he did feel Mrs Forbes to be an uncommonly clever woman. That her cleverness had rather exceeded itself in this matter, he had no way of knowing. All that was now plain to him was that Miss Collins had accused him of 'mocking' her, whereas he had had no such intention. On that account, an apology was long overdue, and George was glad to admit that, since it gave him a pretext for approaching her.

On the next morning he set out for the Rectory without waiting for breakfast, with the consequence that the Collins family was still at its own. Another consequence, more fortunate, was that George's advent had not been observed from the book-room window. When the servant came to the dining-room to say that Mr George Dallow had called upon Miss Collins, Mrs Collins was able to say: "Show him into the drawing-room, Betty. Marcia, go to him there."

It was evident that Marcia wished to do no such thing. Her face had paled and she could not at once move.

"Why should Mr George Dallow intrude upon us at this

time of the day?" began Mr Collins. "I must greet him myself, since he condescends –"

"Go, Marcia," repeated Mrs Collins, in so peremptory a tone that Marcia rose. To her husband she added: "I expect he is come to engage her for a dance this evening. We need not intervene." She hoped that this visit of Mr George's was occasioned by anything so innocuous, but was afraid there might be a message of something amiss at the Hall, such as an illness of Miss Webster, who might have sent for Marcia; whatever it was, Mr Collins's presence could be only a hindrance; and whatever it might prove to be, Mrs Collins awaited it with her usual patience.

"If it is to be called 'intervening' when, under my own roof–" Mr Collins was proceeding as Marcia closed the door of the dining-room in trepidation, thankful that her father preferred to harangue her mother rather than to follow herself; she did not for a moment believe that Mr George proposed to dance with her; for the far greater proposal he was come to make, she was more than unprepared.

Pale-faced and hesitant, she entered the drawing-room to see him standing in the window. Against its light, she could not discern the expression of his face, but when he stepped forward, she noticed that he too was pale. He said, rapidly:

"I was not mocking you. I am come to apologise. I am very sorry. I was sincere. I have been a coward. I am an unmannerly idiot. I wish you could forgive me. I came in a hurry – Oh, I planned what I would say, but now I forget it. I love you. Now you may mock me in turn. Say what you will to me. I deserve it all."

Marcia could say nothing. The room was cold, the fire not yet lighted. She was shivering. George stepped back and said:

"I deserve too that you should not speak to me. But I

thank you for hearing me. I hope you can understand that I was too hasty. I was in earnest. I had thought you were to marry Robert. But for this long while you have been growing dearer to me. I want you to believe that, but I am explaining it all so ill. D – it, excuse me – I am sorry."

Marcia's agitation was a little calmed by her compassion for his. "Do not be so distressed," she said, her voice faint. "It is good of you to come –"

"It is good of you to receive me, and now you may tell me that I am a fool and a plague, and refuse me, and I shall have made matters no worse, but if you will not accept me, and I cannot hope for that, you will accept my apology, and my promise to love you always, for there can be no one else who ... I am saying it all wrong ..."

"Do I understand," Marcia asked, incredulous, "that you wish to make me a ... proposal ..."

"Yes, I am glad you understand, when I am so clumsy, but if you will not hear my offer, I shall apologise for that too."

Marcia's face now took on a deep colour. "I am sorry that I was so ready to take offence," she said. "I could not believe that you were not joking, and did not believe ... Cannot believe, that you now mean – I do not say that you are insincere ..."

"You find my proposal offensive."

Breathless, Marcia after a moment managed to utter: "No ... Not at all offensive ... I am ..." She did not know what she was; but her face, as she raised it to him, cheeks flushed and eyes sparkling with tears, supplied evidence more convincing than any word, that she found his proposal far from offensive to her.

Mrs Forbes had been right: Miss Collins returned his affection. This recognition dispelled George's awkwardness into rapture. They were both, for some moments, caught up in such shared delight that the drawing-room glowed with warmth. Both were astonished by happiness, and remained suspended in it until voices from the hallway reminded them of the rest of the world. Mr Collins was complaining:

"... No, my dear, it is not fitting that my daughter receive gentlemen alone, under my roof. I insist on an explanation—" And, against some protest of Mrs Collins's, the door of the drawing-room was flung open.

The explanation, which George joyfully gave, astounded both Mr and Mrs Collins as fully as it had their daughter. Mrs Collins studied George's face in only an instant's doubt, before being forced to admit that she saw before her a young man very much in love; Marcia's face allowed as little doubt. Mrs Collins's pleasure and relief were heartfelt. She had not conceived of any such a match for her daughter, but to see Marcia so happy was her first satisfaction on hearing the news.

Mr Collins was in this moment to be pitied. He had allowed himself to become so accustomed to disappointment, that he could expect nothing else. All he felt was that his daughter had betrayed him, just as his son had, in concealing from him her intentions; his children were deceitful as well as insurbordinate.

"It is considered correct," he pronounced, as soon as Mrs Collins had released Marcia from an embrace of tender congratulation and shaken George almost as warmly by the hand, "that a suitor approach the father of his intended bride, to seek permission before making his application. I have no wish to be thought presumptuous, but due respect must be accorded to my cloth, if not to my paternal status."

"I do not think, my love," Mrs Collins interposed, "that we need to stand on any such ceremony with Mr George, when he and his family are already so well known to us."

"My family will be as pleased as surprised, sir, when I tell them of my good fortune," declared George. "I shall tell my father at once, and then we shall announce the engagement at the ball this evening, and surprise everyone."

Marcia protested. "Oh, no, I beg you – Let us have no great affair made of it, with so many people present. I should be overcome – to draw so much attention."

George, expecting as ever his own way, was for a moment a little cast down; but Mr Collins performed his first useful function as prospective father-in-law by saying. "Marcia, I trust you will not let Mr George find you as intractable and stubborn as I myself have found you. Show your grateful spirit by agreeing humbly with his plan."

"No, certainly," cried George at once, "we shall not make an announcement tonight, if you do not wish it. Do not disturb yourself. We shall keep our secret until tomorrow, and I shall then speak to my father."

Marcia's loving glance told her grateful spirit.

"In any case," Mrs Collins mentioned, "the ball is in honour of Captain and Mrs Godfrey, and it is they who should claim attention."

"That is true. Proper deference should be accorded to those to whom it is due," said Mr Collins. "Let nothing be done in haste. I myself, consulted over none of this, would be obliged, sir, were you to favour me with an interview, in order to discuss your request for my daughter's hand and the circumstances of your condition of life."

Upon this, George recollected that he was even now expected at the Hall to assist with the arrangements for tonight's ball, and he took his leave, assuring Mr Collins that a formal interview should take place as soon as possible. Mr Collins retired to his book-room to dwell upon the shocks and deceits practised upon him by his family, while

Marcia and her mother enjoyed a conference in which happiness grew only gradually out of their astonishment. Marcia, gently reproved for concealing from her mother the strength of her feeling for George Dallow, protested that she had concealed it even from herself. All that day passed in a dream from which she tried to wake herself by saying: "He cannot love me. I cannot believe it." But the dream would not be broken. Mrs Collins, for her part, was slow to adduce the benefits that would accrue to her daughter; to be potential mistress at Teverton Hall, an estate several times as large as Longbourn, as well as to have a husband so vigorous, amiable and cheerful – these blessings Mrs Collins did not envy Marcia, but rejoiced in for her; for her own husband's immediate depression of mind she was not at present sorry, since to have him exulting in Marcia's success would have been more trying to her, and to the Dallows.

The day passed quietly at the Rectory, but when it was time to dress for the ball, Mr Collins, in spite of himself, revived. A social event he always found stimulating and, in preparing for this excursion, he seemed to have forgotten about Marcia's engagement, along with his other manifold sorrows. He exhorted his wife and daughter as usual in the conduct he expected of them and had them wait in the hallway as he ran from window to door, warning the servant to have the carriage ready to depart on the instant chosen; it was important to be neither early, nor late; as other carriages began to pass up the lane, he ordered Mrs Collins and Marcia to take their seats. "Now!" he cried, at last, darting out. "That was the Paveys' carriage – Be quick, man, turn out behind it, we shall arrive directly behind the Paveys; that will do very well."

This manoeuvre had one result that Mr Collins could not have contrived. Robert Pavey, who had approached this evening's festivity in no mood for it, was received in the hallway of the manor house along with his father and mother just as the Collinses followed. He saw George Dallow hasten forward and say something to Miss Collins that caused her to draw back from him, raising her hand as if to defend herself.

A pent-up dissatisfaction in Robert seized upon release. He strode to George and said, angrily: "George, have the goodness to leave Miss Collins alone!"

"Why should I do that?" asked George amazed.

"Because I know that you have offended her in some way, and I will not allow you to do so again."

"By what right do you interfere?"

"I have the right of a friend. I am a better friend to her than you are and I will not see you molest her."

George, who had been annoyed by Robert's tone, could now not but laugh. Robert laid his hand on George's shoulder crying:

"Do not dare to laugh at me!"

The brawl was drawing an audience; people gathered round; Marcia's dismay was evident; she was becoming the centre of attention in a way more unfortunate than she had anticipated. George, while shouting to Robert: "Take your hands off me, sir!" at the same time noticed her distress, and added to her in a lower voice:

"I shall have to tell him, to quiet him; may I?"

Marcia nodded, unable to speak, and George shaking off Robert's hand bade him: "We must not, either of us, torment Miss Collins in company. Come outside with me." And he led the way out of doors for privacy, although from Robert's expression it could have been for physical assault. So at any rate thought Philippa, who ran through into the drawing-room to the peril of her carefully dressed hair, calling out:

"What an uproar is here! George has called Robert Pavey outside and they are fighting!"

Mrs Forbes, standing with Silvia, saw that while Philippa seemed not displeased by her own announcement, Silvia had paled in horror. "Do not be afraid," Mrs Forbes cautioned her. "I am sure George is the stronger. Who is Robert Pavey?"

Philippa replied for Silvia: "He is a friend of George's in Fraxted, or he was. One could hardly say so at this moment."

Corinna exclaimed: "I will not have my ball ruined by quarrels and fighting before it is begun! Thomas," she appealed to her husband, "go and stop them."

That warrior obediently marched off to enter the fray and there was a general movement towards the scene of battle. But already George and Robert were re-entering the house, smiling and apparently on better terms than they had been for a long while.

"Oh, they are friends again," remarked Philippa, disappointed.

Everyone else was much relieved, and Robert not least. It had taken but a few moments for George's explanation of the state of affairs between Miss Collins and himself, and of her desire for secrecy this evening. Robert, astonished as anyone by the engagement, was glad of it. George had lifted from his own conscience the reproach of trifling with Miss Collins's affections; for if they had been, all along, as Robert could well believe, directed towards George, then she had been in no serious danger from himself. And George, admittedly in love, was so mellowed and genial that Robert let the old habit of friendship reassert itself. For this interval he even forgot Miss Webster, in his haste to go to Miss Collins, whisper that he offered his hearty congratulations but would not betray her, and solicit the first two dances. George, his happiness even increased by Robert's goodwill, went to make the same request of Silvia; and Silvia, with no idea of why George should be in such high good humour, was nonetheless pleased by it and laughed with him as they passed down the set. Mrs Forbes, watching their gaiety, dared to hope that matters had come right between them.

Her satisfaction was destroyed two hours later, when Mr Collins placed himself beside her on a window-seat as she was enjoying a pause of rest and reflection. Mr Collins was by now exhilarated by the company and prepared to perform his duty of conversation. Since many of those he knew tended to slip away from him after a bow of greeting, he directed his favours upon this solitary stranger and introduced himself with his habitual humble apologies for so doing; continuing:

"I find such occasions as this not unpleasant, indeed, agreeable, and not unbecoming to one of my calling, provided that the bounds of decorum are not overstepped, which in the case of my patron and his charming family is very little to be feared. There was some indiscretion in the manner of a marriage, not long ago, of which you may have heard ill-natured reports, but, apparently, all is forgiven, which is commendable and according to Biblical admonition, provided that the indiscretion has not attained the dimensions of a public scandal." Mrs Forbes seeming to agree with all he said – though in truth, she had fixed an agreeable smile upon her face and was thinking of Silvia – Mr Collins went on, through praise of his patron and all his family, to talk himself into a frame of mind as elated as it had previously been depressed. His patron's good wine, of which Mr Collins had, within the bounds of decorum, imbibed, may have accounted for the glowing picture he now painted of his son's management of the large estate in

Hertfordshire that his father was upon the point of inheriting, and of his daughter's splendid future as mistress of all the magnificence of the mansion in which he and his auditor were privileged to find themselves this evening –

"Your daughter?" echoed Mrs Forbes, not understanding. "I have met her, I think. She is a friend of Silvia –"

"She is, I must in all modesty reveal to you, ma'am, the affianced bride of Mr George Dallow. We are not speaking of it yet, I recall, but you will respect my confidence."

"But that is incredible!" cried Mrs Forbes. "We have heard nothing of it." She heard, now, enough to alarm her; Mr Collins was, she had to believe, not inventing the story. She listened to little more of his attestation, being occupied in casting back her mind over her talk with George on the preceding evening. No 'young lady' had been named; was it possible that all she had said George had taken to refer to some other young lady than Silvia? She had to fear so. Her interference had been disastrous. Instead of saving Silvia from another betrayal, she had brought it upon her. Her contrition was painful, but her pity for Silvia even more so.

Looking about for Silvia, she saw her dancing with Walter and saw that Silvia appeared unusually tired. George, dancing with a young lady in blue, was beaming still. Could Silvia have heard the news? If no one were more discreet than Miss Collins's father, possibly she had. But Mrs Forbes had no opportunity to ask. She suffered for the rest of the evening and had to wait until Silvia had retired, before finding her alone.

"Are you very tired, my dear? Let me help you unpin your hair."

"Yes, I am a little tired. The ball seemed so long." It had seemed so to Silvia, because Robert Pavey had not once asked her to dance.

"Please tell me what is troubling you?"

"It is nothing. I am only tired."

"You have heard nothing – no news – to distress you?"

"No; what should I have heard?"

Mrs Forbes did not shrink from telling her, though delicately, the news she had received from Mr Collins. Silvia, to her amazement but to her relief, was delighted.

"George and Miss Collins! I am so glad. She is a sweet, deserving girl, and I am sure George will make an excellent husband for her, if he sets his mind to it. He is kind at heart, do you not think so?"

Mrs Forbes, reassured, was still puzzled. Whom, then, did Silvia love? Brushing Silvia's hair, as she had brushed it when Silvia was a little girl, Mrs Forbes reminded herself: I must be more careful in my interference, but I still feel that there may be need of it.

NINETEEN

George Dallow was, by the morning after the ball, quite accustomed to the notion of himself as a bridegroom and underestimated the effect that his announcement might have on his family; so he treated their objections casually. These were, however, not too serious. Miss Collins had, in the eyes of Mr and Mrs Dallow, everything to recommend her except for beauty, wealth and connections. This apart, they were ready to love her for George's sake and, when she visited the Hall, and they saw her afresh through George's eyes, she was seen to be quite pretty, very well mannered, sensible and – In short, they stopped counting up her attributes, and accepted her.

George visited Mr Collins and returned home to say: "Father, is there not some living in your gift, say a thousand miles off, to which Marcia's father could be preferred?" The Dallows, upon the whole, still found Mr Collins laughable.

Mr Dallow's caution to his son, at first, had been to say: "It does not do to decide things in a hurry," and then to proceed: "Well, we shall set the wedding for April, when I am back from Carthage, and in the meantime you must have the farmhouse at Welton done up for you, for it is better that young people have a place of their own, and it is a fine house of its kind. How lucky that it stands vacant.

You must take Samson to be housekeeper, for she knows your ways, and your mother can spare her." With other examples of deciding nothing in haste, he had set matters in train in no time. Marcia, when she saw the house at Welton, was again incredulous of her good fortune; the rooms were larger and brighter than those of the Rectory, and the house, standing midway between Teverton and Fraxted, could not have been more convenient.

"I cannot yet believe," she told George, "that these things are happening to me."

George could not believe, in retrospect, that he had not entertained the idea of marriage much sooner. The state had, he now saw, every advantage – marriage to Marcia in particular; but, in general, he advocated it to everyone not yet entered upon it. Since the night of the ball, he and Robert had resumed their old relationship and to Robert George gave sage counsel.

"You see how it is with Corinna," he said as they were out shooting together. "She has not once been freakish or out of temper since she was here, and that is because her Thomas keeps her happy. As for myself, when I am settled at Welton with Marcia, upon my oath, you will never hear me swearing and shouting again. Why do you not marry? It would be the best thing to cure your mopishness. How should you like to marry Jane, or Philippa?"

Robert thanked George, but did not suppose either lady would want him.

"Oh, but they would – any girl would. What have you against you? Good enough looks and family, respectable profession, and you can sing."

"I do not think that adequate to the situation."

"Ha – So there is a situation, is there? I might have guessed it. Whom does it involve – I know: Elizabeth Browne. Swear it is not?"

"I swear nothing. Look, here come the others," said Robert gladly, as Henry Webster and Thomas Godfrey, who had drawn the woods from another direction, appeared at the top of the ride.

The party at Teverton was soon to disperse. The military gentlemen must return to duty and Mrs Forbes to her own plans, for she must sell her house and make many other dispositions before her wedding. For that event Silvia was to go to Bath, but until then she preferred to remain at Teverton. No one could persuade her that she must find winter in the country dull. Yet, she did not seem in quite such fine health as hitherto. Tiredness from the ball could not have persisted for so long. Mrs Forbes began to think she had perhaps better take Silvia to Gibraltar; Henry thought he had better take her to Bath himself and introduce Richardson to her; Jane and Philippa thought they should compel her to learn to ride; Mrs Dallow thought of a dozen new specifics. No one thought in this connection of Robert Pavey, who, although he rode and shot with George again, did not visit the Hall, Nor had he, for some time; the books of songs lay by the pianoforte and only Silvia turned the pages.

Her feeling for Robert Pavey was a lack; she missed him; she was incomplete. She might have told Mrs Forbes of this, but why recount so negative a sensation? Besides, Mrs Forbes did not know Robert Pavey; they must have been introduced at the ball, but neither had seen reason to form acquaintance. So Silvia was listless, and wanting in appetite, and fancied that perhaps she was not quite well, as they told her; they did not explain to her that she was in love.

She did one day, however, conceive a plan that she must carry out in secret and that required great daring; the project restored some energy to her. On the next morning,

when she was in Fraxted with Mrs Forbes and Jane, she
invented an errand that would take her to the far end of the
town; and, dispensing with the escort of Mrs Forbes, from
whom the secret must especially be kept, Silvia asked her
way to the offices of Pavey and Son, where she timidly
requested an interview.

She need not have been afraid. Mr Pavey was kindness
itself, drawing up a chair for her beside his own, offering
her wine and setting her at her ease:

"Naturally, a young lady such as yourself does not
understand these legal matters. I, at my age and with my
experience, still find them difficult. Particularly, I might
add, in the instance of your family. I wish Mr Dallow
himself would honour me with a visit. I am grateful that
you are come. Now, my dear," with paternal familiarity,
"in what way can I assist you?"

Silvia hesitantly explained. She knew, she said, that
while she was in Mrs Forbes's care, that lady had received a
regular allowance for Silvia's needs. Would it be possible
for that to be continued, or some similar allowance to be
made, after Mrs Forbes's marriage? How could it be
arranged, and could it be afforded out of Silvia's income?

"Certainly it could be afforded," said Mr Pavey with a
smile. He pondered the question, then suggested that a
total sum be transferred to Mrs Forbes, under the nature of
a wedding gift –

"Yes – That, she would be forced to accept!" cried
Silvia.

"Quite so. Then she could invest or spend it as she liked.
It should be placed solely in her own name," added Mr
Pavey, reflecting that, should Admiral So-and-so turn out
to be as improvident as some naval men he had heard of, his
wife (or widow) need not suffer from it. "As your
guardian," he continued, "Mr Dallow must sign any deed

of gift, and we shall see to it that he does, before he runs off to Morocco or where else. If need be, I shall come myself to Teverton, pistol in hand."

"Oh, I hope that will not be necessary!"

"No, no. I was making a little joke. Now let us review the state of your finances at this time. I have not the figures here –" Ringing a bell, he asked the messenger who entered: "Will you please ask Mr Robert to come in, and bring with him the boxes relevant to Dallow – Not, of course, all of them; the box marked Webster, in that section."

Mr Pavey sent for his son because he knew that Miss Webster was acquainted with Robert and would be less shy with him than with the frightening Mr Grimsby or other elderly clerks. Little did he imagine the shyness that afflicted his young client when Robert appeared, nor did he, intent on unlocking the deed-box, observe his son's discomposure as Robert beheld Miss Webster seated beside his father's desk.

"Thank you, Robert," said Mr Pavey. "Take a chair, please. Miss Webster is consulting us over a scheme she has in mind." In his precise lawyer's prose he outlined the process by which a deed of gift should be made, to the complete inattention of both his companions. This confrontation, so unexpected, gave each a sense of unreality; their eyes met, turned away, and met again, as it were through the screen of Mr Pavey's voice. Their wordless communication brought them strangely close; had they been able to speak, they might have found nothing to say. There was an exchange of feeling; both drew slightly back from it.

What had prevented their coming together? On Robert's side, his initial worship of Silvia as of some remote ideal; on Silvia's, her diffidence, her simple shyness and an inner persuasion, gained from who knew where, that she must become a woman of the world and seek not to depend on anyone. But then, Robert was a natural worshipper, and she naturally dependent; the qualities that would have made them perfectly adapted to one another were precisely those that kept them apart. As Mr Pavey prosed on, their exchanged glances were of mingled understanding, regret, sympathy and a lingering relinquishment.

"Now, to review, as I promised, the present state of your affairs," Mr Pavey said more briskly, unfolding a document and rousing Silvia to turn to him. Robert too assumed a more lawyer-like expression. His father read patiently through lists of figures and records of investments and titles to lands, laying down one document upon another and finally glancing up to say informally: "And you will want to know, my dear, what all that amounts to in simple language?" He told her.

"Could you please repeat that to me, Mr Pavey?" asked Silvia. And when he had done so:

"I had no idea that I had so much money as that!" she exclaimed with a naïveté that made Mr Pavey smile.

"It may be as well," he said, beginning to gather the documents into the box, "that you should know. I am not querying the wisdom of your guardians, who have not explained matters to you. It may be that they too are unaware of the extent of your fortune. When I say that it is as well that you know, I mean that you should be warned against the dangers attending a young lady in your position. It can be, paradoxically, a misfortune for a young girl to possess a fortune. You will understand that it can attract, if I may speak intimately, candidates for her hand in marriage who have that fortune in view. What I have told you may serve to put you on your guard. But to be on your guard against suitors is not agreeable. On the other hand, I have known young men be so afraid to be thought mercenary, that they will not approach a lady they know to be rich. It is a sad thing for a young lady, to suspect any man who seems attracted to her of being either mercenary or a coward."

That one word had a startling effect. Robert had indeed been afraid of approaching Miss Webster in large part because of her wealth; but Mr Pavey had no idea that his son was at all attracted towards Miss Webster. He was innocent of the provocation he gave his son, who astonished him by saying, hotly:

"I am no such coward, Father!"

The other two looked at him, Mr Pavey with legal inscrutability, Silvia with bewilderment. Robert hurried on:

"I have been aware for this long time, as you know, of the extent of Miss Webster's fortune. I admit that it has deterred me from seeking her closer acquaintance. But it is not that alone. It is that I am in every way unworthy of her. I should in no case have presumed to seek her hand. I have wished for nothing more than to be allowed to love her. And so I do – love her. I am sorry she is so rich. But I am not a coward."

"Do I understand from all this," said Mr Pavey in mild perplexity, "that you are making at this moment a proposal of marriage to Miss Webster?"

"No. Yes. – I hardly know –"

"In either case," remarked Mr Pavey drily, "such an interview could more properly be conducted otherwise than in my office, and presence." He looked at Silvia, whose face was lowered and whose hands were twisted together in some anguish. "It would be my suggestion, that you take Miss Webster for a short walk, shall we say into the lime avenue by the river, and resume your utterances in a more becoming privacy."

Robert, in the open air with Miss Webster beside him, could for some time utter nothing. Following his father's advice, at least in part, he led her to the river walk and in faint winter sunshine they paced beneath the frosty twigs of the lime trees. In his agitation he was walking too fast for her, and Silvia, to request his waiting for her, put her hand on his arm. Robert then broke out:

"You take my arm! Does that mean that you ... are not angry?"

"But – Why should I be angry?"

"I did not mean to speak as I did. You must realise that? It was only, that my father stirred me, by referring to cowardice." But now, cooled a little by the air and recollection, he added: "Though probably he did not intend to refer to myself. He was speaking generally?"

"Yes ... You did not mean," asked Silvia in her innocent directness, "to propose marriage to me?"

"My dear Miss Webster," he cried, halting and turning to her, "how can you doubt me? Nothing could be truer to my desire, but I cannot pursue that intention, when I was forced to speak so much ahead of myself, and so awkwardly, and my thoughts are so much in confusion."

"My thoughts, too, are in confusion," Silvia admitted; but he felt her little hand holding closer to his arm, as if she sought his support. It was enough to encourage him to go on:

"Were I to do that ... To ask you to marry me ... When I am more in command of myself and can choose the occasion ... Could I hope ..."

This experimental offer of marriage did nothing to resolve Silvia's confusion. "I wish you would propose to me," she murmured, "when it is convenient to you to do so." Then, appalled by her temerity, she withdrew her hand and turned her colouring face from him.

Robert, in a thrill of hope, recognised the absurdity of his position and the difficult position in which he was placing Miss Webster. He could even laugh a little at himself. Removing his hat, he cried: "Miss Webster, let me strive to make myself clear. Here and now, I make you a resolute request for your hand in marriage." She had, by implication, made herself clear enough to permit this boldness. And now, by putting her hand again on his arm, she indicated what her reply would have been, had she been able to summon speech.

They walked on, lingering, revelling in that peace of being alone together that is the purest pleasure of love. Robert had been thrust into an impetuousness more in George Dallow's character than his own and, now that Miss Webster too was serene again, he was content; they were in no hurry to discuss the future. This happy interlude was terminated only by Silvia's remembering that she was to meet Mrs Forbes and Jane by the market cross at noon. It was already half past noon by the church clock. "I must go!" she cried. "What is the quickest way from her to the market square? They will wonder where I am."

With one steadfast clasp of her hands and few inadequate phrases of his eternal gratitude and devotion, Robert prepared to lead her to the market square. There, when they saw the Teverton carriage awaiting, Silvia said: "I thank you, so much – I must leave you –" and ran off, dispensing with his escort. Arriving at the carriage she was out of breath and apologetic – and, to Mrs Forbes's keen eyes, agitated by more than her running. There were traces of recent tears, but of a more recent cheerfulness, which gave Silvia's countenance a glow that it had not had for a long time.

"My dear," Mrs Forbes half reproached her, "where have you been?"

Silvia now found herself in difficulty. Mrs Forbes must not be allowed to know of the business conducted at the solicitor's. She must not know of Silvia's deed of gift until everything was signed and done, or she would refuse it. So, Silvia could not explain either that she had been with Mr Robert Pavey; the question would be: "How did you come to meet him?" Her simple honesty could not invent any plausible half-truth. She said only: "I am sorry. My ... errand delayed me."

What that errand could have been, Mrs Forbes could only surmise, but with some alarmed curiosity. There was a consciousness in Silvia, a blush and an avoidance of eyes, that defied explanation. And, this time, Mrs Forbes knew herself not mistaken: Silvia had been with someone she loved. Worse: Silvia did not mean to tell her of it.

In Jane's presence Mrs Forbes said no more, but, returned to the Hall, she accompanied Silvia upstairs. "Now that we are in private," she began, "you must please tell me, my dear, what errand you were upon in the town."

"Oh ... I cannot. Please excuse me."

"You cannot confide in *me*? But, Silvia – Why not?"

"Because," said Silvia breaking into tears, "you would try to prevent me from – from what I wish to do."

"You know that I would not do that. When have I ever crossed your interests? Have you ceased to believe that I am your true friend, and love you as a mother? Silvia, trust me. I know that there is someone you love and it breaks my heart that you keep secrets from me. I am certain that you intend to do nothing that would grieve me and I know you incapable of dishonourable action; what can you have to hide?"

By now Silvia was weeping so bitterly that Mrs Forbes pitied her, while recognising that, distressed as she was, Silvia was still not about to make any disclosure. Mrs

Forbes kissed her and left her, to go downstairs and propound to the Dallows the most unlikely theory that Silvia had a clandestine lover in Fraxted, with whom she had this morning kept an assignation. Had anyone, she implored, any idea of who it could be, or what had secretly been happening?

Everyone was incredulous. "Silvia, of all people!" cried Corinna. "Impossible!" And everyone agreed with her.

"But I am sure I am right," Mrs Forbes insisted. "I know Silvia so well, and I know these symptoms. She is keeping from me, as never before, the state of her heart. She is weeping and distraught and says that, were I to find out what she intends to do, I would prevent her. I can not believe that she means to run away ... But what can it then mean?"

"Silvia would not consent to an elopement," said Corinna, her own face colouring as she admitted the comparison. "And she knows no one in Fraxted. Can it be a follower from Bath?"

No one could imagine who Silvia's lover might be. Why did no one think of Robert Pavey? Because, in the general dismay, with talk of assignations and secrets, the family friend Robert did not come into anyone's mind.

It was an unhappy day. Silvia remained upstairs, her tears unceasing. Mrs Dallow went to her with persuasions and possets, but neither to her entreaties did Silvia yield. Among the younger members of the household, opinions were divided; Jane and Philippa were disposed to wish all success to Silvia's escapade, while Henry, and Thomas Godfrey, were zealous to discover and shoot the man in question and rather looked forward to the achievement. At dinner, however, in deference to Mrs Forbes's feelings, the atmosphere was grave. Conversation was confined to safe trivialities.

Silvia did not appear, but, a little later, an unexpected visitor came. The Paveys' carriage drove up and Mr Pavey was announced. He entered the drawing-room, a wallet under his arm, and after greeting the company, said to Mr Dallow:

"I have a document here, sir, that requires your immediate signature."

"Look here, Pavey, this is too bad of you. You are always requiring me to sign documents, but never before have you chased me into my own house, and at this hour of the night. It will wait until I can come to your office."

"It will not wait," said Mr Pavey, sternly. "Take me at once, please, into the library, where we may talk in private. To write your name is the work of a moment, and I must insist that you comply." Mr Pavey himself, it must be admitted, was not without enjoyment of this flagrant bullying of his client. Nor could Mr Dallow in courtesy refuse him, when Mr Pavey in person had made the journey during his own leisure time. The two gentlemen withdrew to the library, followed by a gale of mirth from Mr Dallow's children at his discomfiture.

In only a few minutes, Mr Pavey returned with his wallet again under his arm and Mr Dallow behind him. "Well, so that is settled," said Mr Pavey, now genially smiling. "But is Miss Webster not here? I must tell her that her business is completed."

"Miss Webster is in her room," said Mrs Dallow, wondering. "She is not very well."

"I am sorry to hear that. I particularly wished to see her, of course, to say how glad Mrs Pavey and I are to know of her engagement to our son. Would you, please, convey our –"

"Silvia is engaged to Robert?" cried Corinna, Jane and

Philippa with one voice. Philippa added:

"And are they planning to run away?"

"They had better not," said Robert's father with calm. "Why indeed should they?"

"Robert Pavey!" said Mrs Dallow enlightened. "Of course, there is someone in Fraxted whom she knows. She must have met him this morning."

"Indeed she did," Mr Pavey confirmed. "And this morning, Robert tells us, the proposal was made, in due form, after a little confusion –"

"I am so pleased," Corinna declared. "Robert and she will be so well suited –"

"And they can sing together like birds in a nest," said Philippa the irrepressible, joyful for her cousin. "Henry, you must not shoot him."

"Who is Robert Pavey?" asked Mrs Forbes.

TWENTY

Robert did not delay in calling upon Mr Dallow to ask him formally for Silvia's hand. Mr Dallow gave his consent, adding: "I am glad she is not caught by one of those fortune-hunters."

"I thank you for your implied good opinion, sir."

"Well, and I am sure you do not mean to live off her money, or in any great style."

"No, sir. That would appeal to neither of us. I shall continue in my profession."

Reminded, Mr Dallow said in some glee: "There will be all kinds of bother, with marriage settlements, and that sort of thing, but you and your father can see to it. If there is anything for me to sign, I will do so when I am back from Carthage."

On this same visit to the Hall, Robert re-encountered Mrs Forbes, who did not at first remember, in this radiant young man, the lugubrious gentleman who had been introduced to her at the ball. Silvia, now that the secret of her deed of gift to Mrs Forbes could be disclosed, was as radiant; Mrs Forbes could reprove her only for the magnitude of the gift to herself.

"I declare," said Mrs Dallow, "it is nothing but weddings. Three of my family within a few months, to be take from me!" But Silvia would not be far away, since

Robert was to continue with Pavey and Son; they were looking for a house near Fraxted; and George would be as close to Teverton as Welton. This news, that Miss Webster was to remain in the neighbourhood, pleased Marcia, when she heard it, almost as much as the news of the engagement of Silvia and Robert. "I hope we shall still see each other, and be friends," she said to Silvia.

"Indeed we shall. We shall often be together."

"How pleasant it is, that George and Robert are friends again also. It might have been difficult, had they not been."

"Were they ever not?" asked Silvia in surprise.

She left for Bath with Mrs Forbes, as there was no private reason for her lingering at Teverton now that she was sure of Robert's affection, and she wished to be as much as possible with Mrs Forbes before their separation. The Godfreys, and Henry Webster, departed with them and Mr Dallow's journey was immiment. On the eve of this, one embarrassment arose, which threatened the prevailing happiness.

Mr Collins's improvement of spirits, since the evening of the ball, had been maintained even when the effects of Mr Dallow's wine had passed off. He was now as elated as he had been dejected and, far from lamenting his disappointments, recognised that his life was crowned with a multitude of blessing, not least among these his children. His gratitude to his patron and to his deity made him as insufferable as ever. He called at the manor to express his deep sense of obligation to Mr Dallow – for what, his verbosity did not illuminate – when Mr Dallow was in the midst of packing his books, and set that gentleman back in his preparations by a valuable two hours.

"Is that man to be always here in future?" Mr Dallow complained when at last Mr Collins had bowed himself away. "He seems to think himself a member of the family, obsequious as he is about it, and so I suppose he is. George, you must get him to call at Welton, when you are there, instead of at the Hall. I cannot do with him."

"Frankly, sir, no more can I."

"That was no bad idea of yours, that we might find him another living. I wish I knew of one."

Mr Dallow did not know that such an idea had not been George's alone. Mrs Collins had perceived that her husband might be a source of real tribulation to Marcia, in her new connections. It was very well to laugh at the Rector during a family dinner-party but the joke was not one that George could properly share with his wife, the joke's own loyal daughter. Mrs Collins knew that no remonstrations of her own would have effect on her husband. He would feel that he owed it to the dignity of his cloth to be always in and out of Teverton Hall and Welton House with fulsome representations of respect and self-congratulation. The only remedy would be his removal from the district.

The sacrifice to Mrs Collins, of Marcia's company, would be great, but for Marcia's sake she would attempt to make it. She wrote to her friends in Derbyshire, as the only people she knew who might have sufficient influence, couching her request in terms that, as usual, sought no pity. After announcing the good news of Marcia's forthcoming marriage, she added that, since William was now settled at Longbourn, the Rectory at Teverton was larger than Mr and Mrs Collins required in the way of a residence; and that Mr Dallow, generous as he was as a patron, was so often absent, that Mr Collins felt called upon to bear too much of the benevolent work of the district. Mrs Collins re-wrote the letter many times, still suspecting that her friend would read between the lines of it; and her friend, easily doing so, begged her husband to seek some means of transferring Mr Collins to another living, for Mrs Collins's sake.

The means, by great good fortune, was soon found. Another friend had at his disposal a living in Bedfordshire with a stipend equal to that of Teverton, a well appointed house but neglected gardens, and a patron who was a titled gentleman and, according to the report of Mrs Collins's friend, 'a somewhat unapproachable character'. It was to this last challenge that Mr Collins finally responded. At first he had been indignant at any suggestion of his moving to another parish and forfeiting the glories of Teverton Hall after so many years of striving to attain them. His renewed energies did, however, welcome an outlet; Mr Dallow had no title; to lay out other gardens would be an agreeable exertion. In the end Mr Collins decided to seek, as he felicitiously phrased it, fresh woods and pastures new.

Mrs Collins resigned herself to parting from Marcia and to witnessing her husband's attentions to the unapproachable patron. It was everything to her that her children were happy. William came to Marcia's wedding, and thereafter wrote faithfully to his mother. George and Marcia established themselves very comfortably at Welton and that autumn, when Mr Dallow was back from Spain, Robert and Silvia were married and settled in a house near Fraxted that, modest as it was in view of Silvia's wealth, suited them both better than any spendid mansion. In the course of time Jane and Philippa married and, although they lived at a greater distance, the family bonds of the Dallows remained as strong. At Christmas, and on every occasion to be celebrated, there was a gathering, always happy and, as children appeared, as tumultuous as ever, at Teverton Hall.